Faceless Artists is published by Darker Intentions Press,
POB 569, Freehold Township, New Jersey, USA.

Printed in the United States of America

Layout and Design by Darker Intentions Press. Individual drawings and stories by students of the Academy Street Firehouse Program.

ISBN 0-9827597-3-8

ISBN13 978-0-9827597-3-8

Publisher's Note

This book is a work of fiction. Names, characters, people, places and incidents are either the product of the individual author's imagination or used fictitiously, and any resemblance to actual persons, living or dead, business establishments, events, or location is merely coincidental.

Acknowledgements

This book would not have been possible without the talent of the students at the Academy Street Firehouse. I am forever grateful to them for letting me into their lives and sharing their talent.

This project would not have come to pass without an ART START grant from the Newark Arts Council. I would personally like to thank Ms. Armisey Smith, talented artist and Art Education Director of the Newark Arts Council. Her talent, kindness and mentorship was invaluable. Many thanks also to Mr. Linwood J. Oglesby, Executive Director of the Newark Arts Council.

I cannot say enough about Ms. Regina E. Fitch, Youth Program Director at the Academy Street Firehouse, and her staff for their assistance in helping me produce this literary/art project. Without her hard work and support, Faceless Artists could not have come into being. Many thanks from the bottom of my heart to Ms. Joshshea Bonds, Ms.Chante Bryant, and the many volunteers, interns and students who assisted me in the classroom.

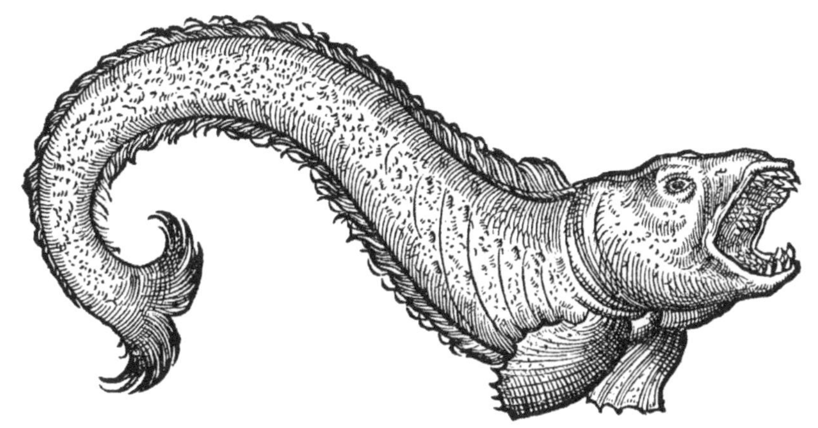

TABLE OF CONTENTS

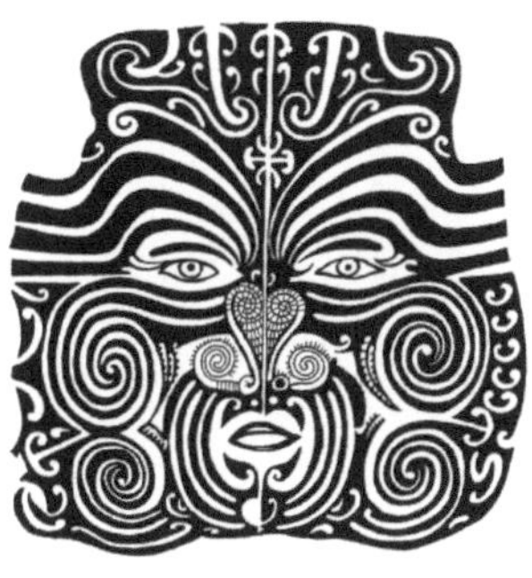

“To send light into the darkness of men’s hearts - such is the duty of the artist.”

-Robert Schumann (German composer, 1810-1856)

FACELESS ARTISTS

DARKER INTENTIONS PRESS

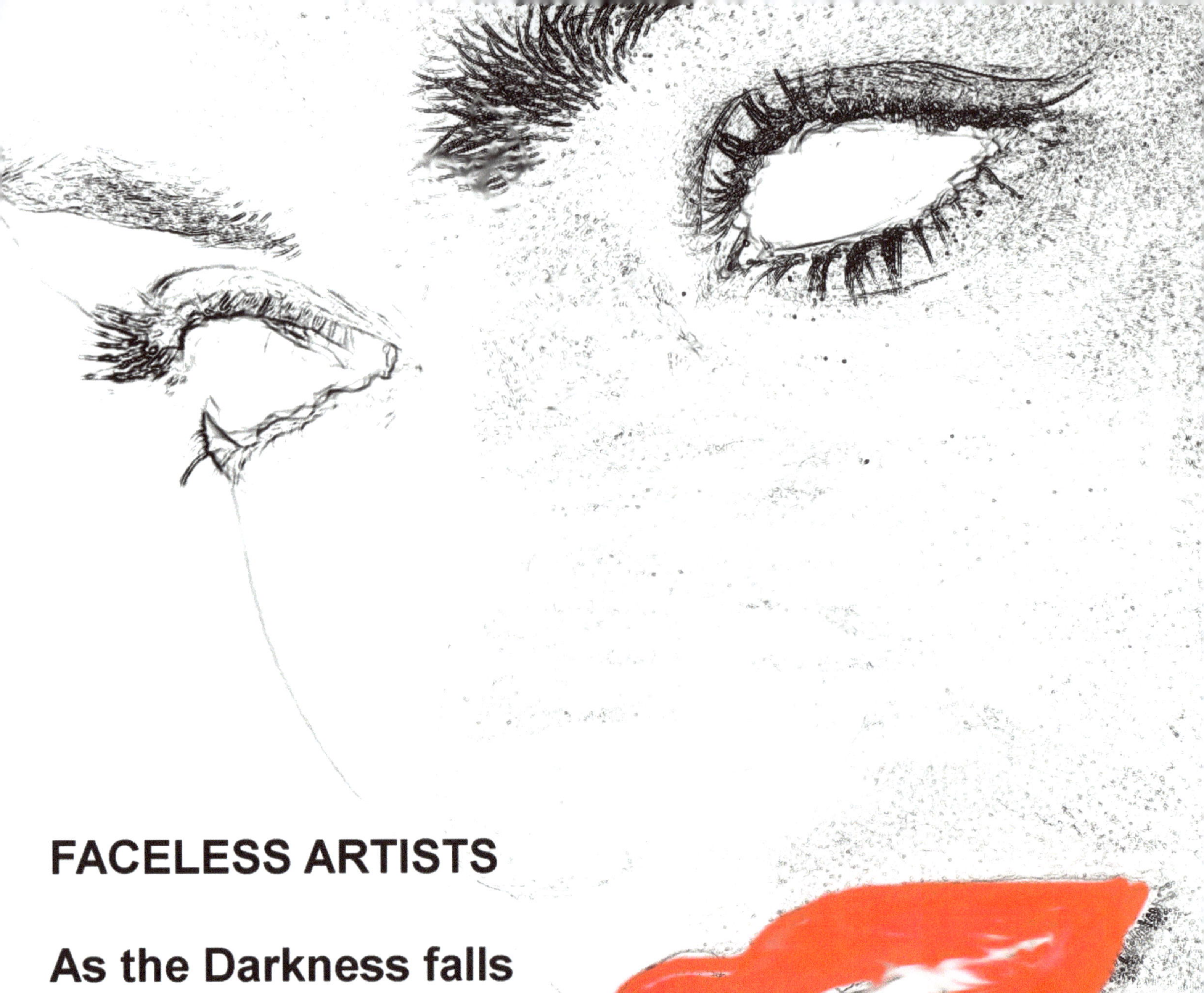

FACELESS ARTISTS

As the Darkness falls
We are spirits of the wind
Bound by no walls
We live in Shadows
Around the corners
We hide

Maybe you'll see us
Maybe you won't
Though we exist
Meet us at Midnight
The Faceless Artists

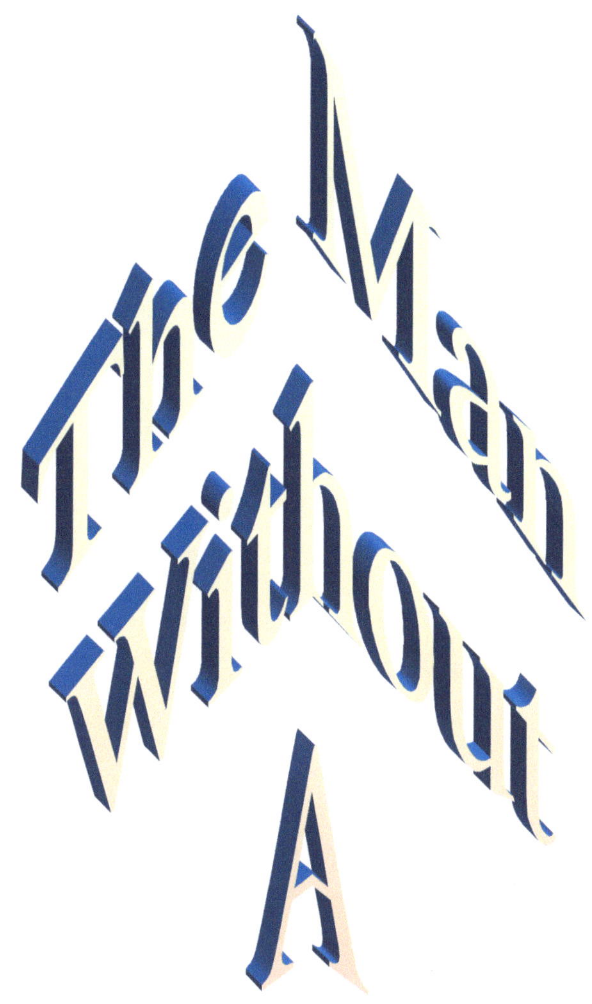

Soul

by Davon Moody

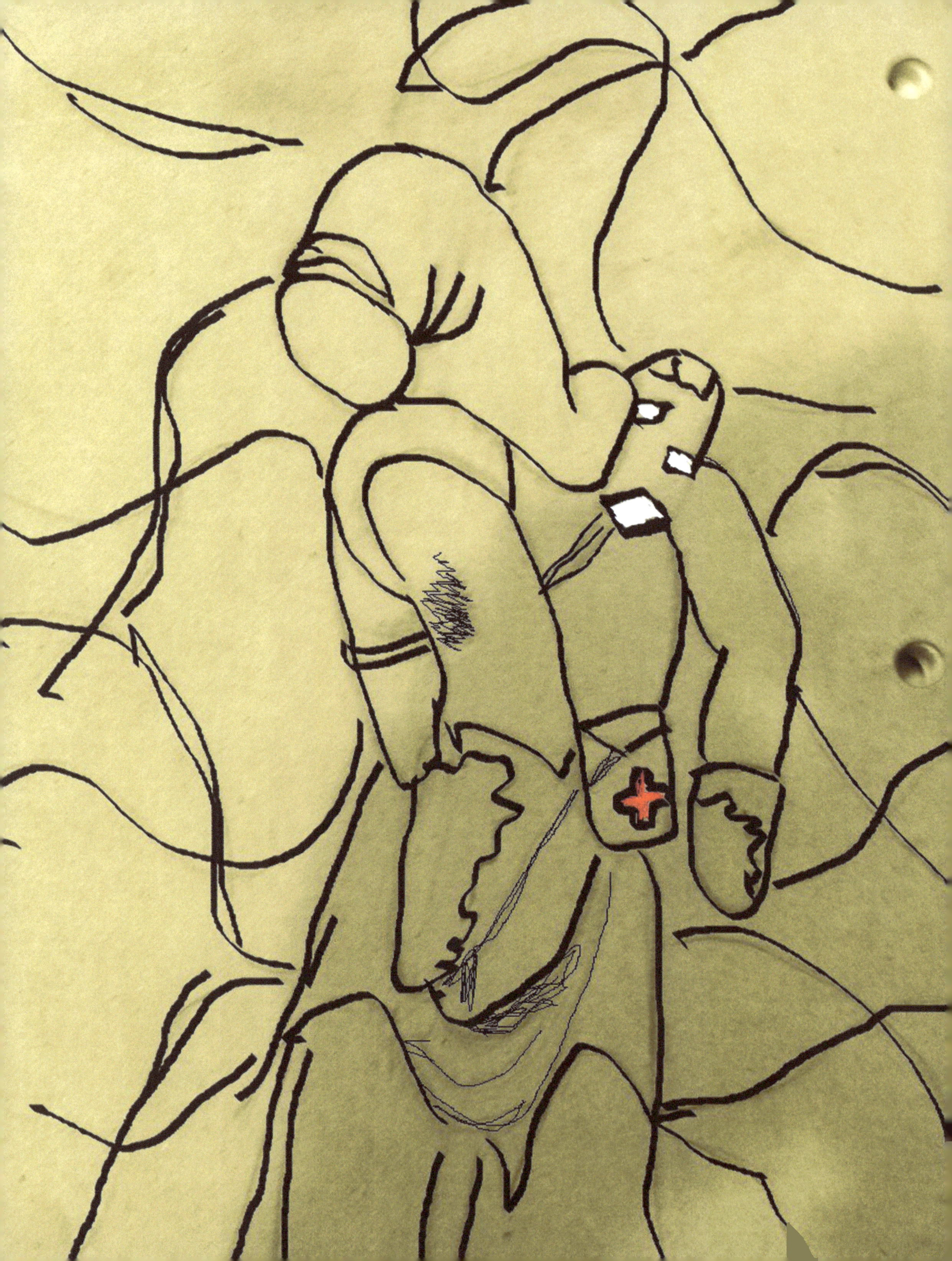

Its purpose? Trying to gain its soul back and come back to LIFE.

Its weapons of choice? It uses the lines of its soul to protect itself, sort of like a bubble.

Its story: I come from Hell. Once human, I lost my soul years ago. But I have been given a chance to earn it back and live once again.

My name is best left unknown.

My purpose is to earn my soul back from the thing that took it from me. I don't need weapons other than the lines that protect me. It surrounds my entire shape.

I am going to do whatever it takes for me to get my life back. Failing is not an option and I must kill whoever is assigned to me in order to be free…

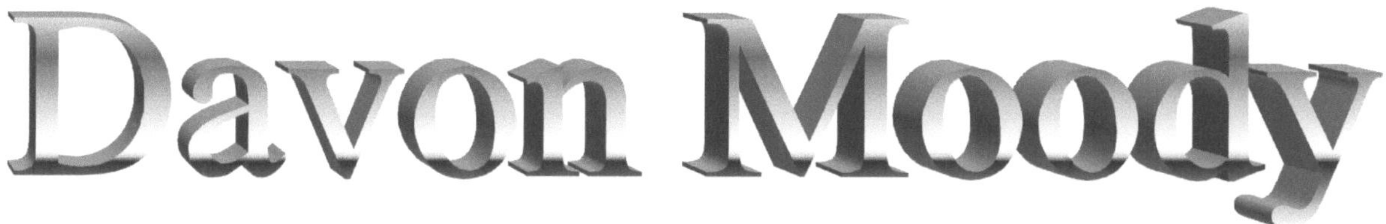

How is your Soul doing these days?

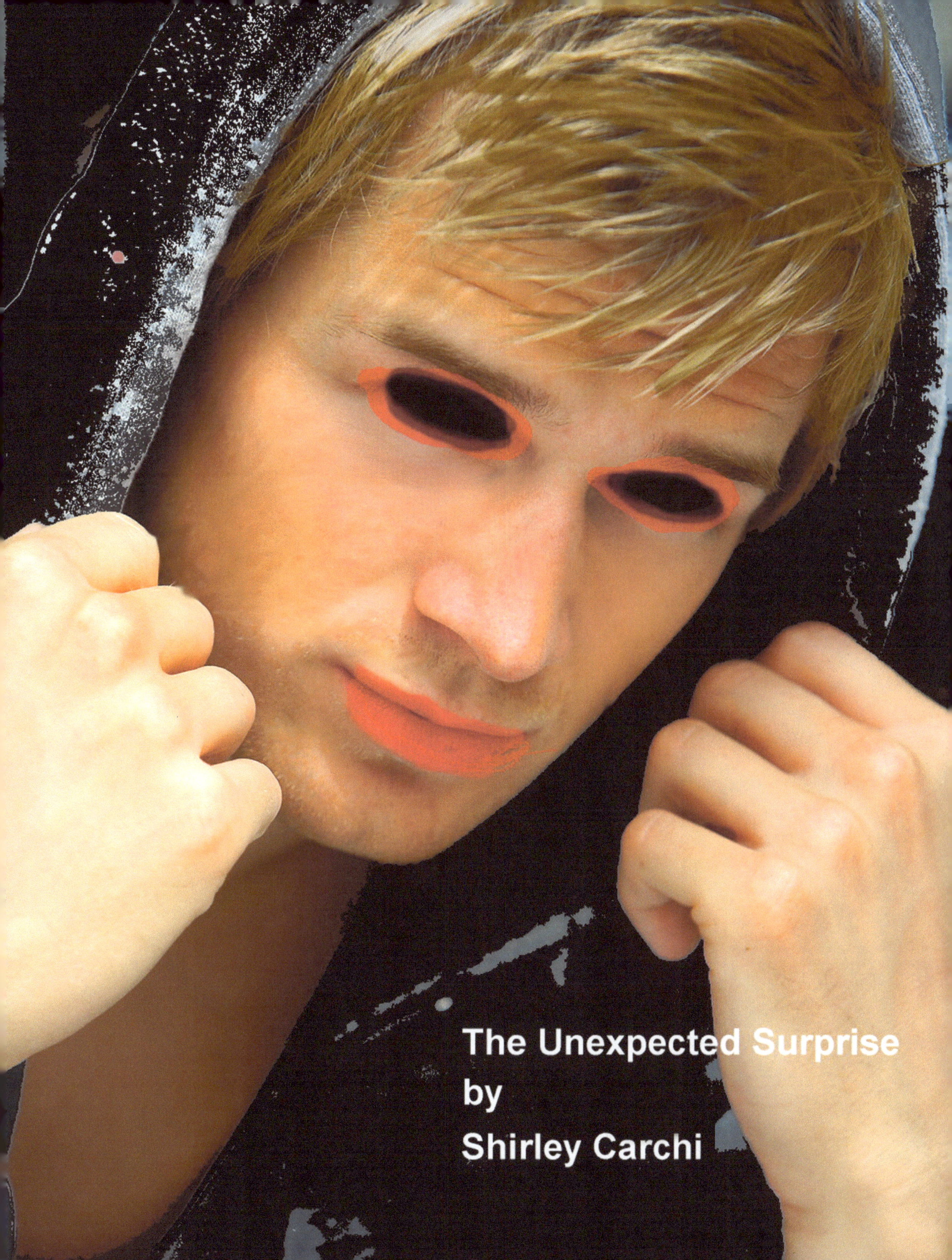
The Unexpected Surprise
by
Shirley Carchi

Who is that? This was question that crossed my head millions of times as I ran. I had been running for what seemed like hours without any end. My goal: to reach the coffin ahead of me and see who the person in it was. The faster I ran, the farther away the coffin seemed. I never got close enough to even touch it.

When my feet finally grew tired, they stopped and my body dropped to the floor. My bones felt like paper and for as much as I tried to get up, I couldn't. Suddenly I felt a drop of water on my arms and then the sound of thunder approached. I wrapped my arms around my legs and put my head down. Huge tears formed in my eyes and immediately fell as I blink, caressing my cheeks lightly until they finally stopped at my neck.

I tried to hold the tears but for some reason they seemed inevitable. I tried to understand my reasons for crying; my reasons for stopping, but it could not fit into my head. My thoughts were interrupted by the sounds of sobs, and it took me a minute to realize that they were my own.

"Why?" I yelled as I looked up to the sky, still sobbing.

I couldn't figure out my own feelings. They were a mixture of anger, sadness, disappointment, and depression. Suddenly, I no longer felt rain drops and I lifted my head and looked straight and the coffin was still there. I stood up and as I did, the sun began to rise and all of the rain clouds began to vanish.

I ran. Faster than I had ever before. I did not know where my energy had come from but it was not important right now. The coffin no longer moved farther away as I got near. It remained in the same place until I finally approached it. My hands and body began to tremble as I neared it, reaching to touch it. My eyes grew in shock and my mouth let out a scream when I saw the person's face. My father looked straight into my eyes. Blood covered his body and worms were eating his flesh, only face was clear. As tears formed, I pressed my head against his chest, not caring about the worms. There was no heart beat, no breathing, he was gone. I lifted my head and slowly brought my fingers , which were shaking uncontrollably, toward his eyes. I took a last look at them, before closing them. They had no expression. For a second I thought I saw a hint of sadness, I thought it was just me but then I heard him whisper, "I'm fine, just take care of yourself, be careful," and his eyes closed.

I heard myself say softly, " Rest in peace Daddy, I love you," as I hugged him for the last time. Then I began to scream and I could not stop myself.

"Get up, get up," a soft voice in the background. I felt someone shaking me slightly. My eyes immediately opened a little as my felt freezing cold water run through it. Now I felt that the shaking was not soft, but hard. I heard myself screaming and as my eyes opened wider each second I began to see what was going on.

My mother was stood next to me, shaking me to wake up, her eyes worried, tears forming. My father (well technically step dad) stood alongside of her with the same worried look as my mother, which surprised me. In his hand was a bucket.

When my eyes were fully opened and I was back to reality, the screaming stopped. I reached up to feel my face which wet, but not only from the water that I had been soaked in earlier, but from tears that were still falling. I focused my eyes on my crying mother as she sat down next to me and hugged me. My dad put his hand on my head and petted it softly, something that he had not done since I was five.

Tonight no questions were asked. This had been occurring for a month now, once or even twice a week. My biological father appeared in my dreams. In each of the dreams he was dead in a coffin and he would tell me to take care of myself and I screamed when he closed his eyes.

My father died when I was two years old. Being so young, I do not remember him at all. The only memory that I have of him is pictures of my baptism and his and my mothers wedding. My father's death affected me in so many ways. I wouldn't eat or sleep; all I did was ask where he was. He spoiled me in every way possible. I was at his funeral, but being so small, I thought he was sleeping, and I would tell everyone to be quite because daddy's sleeping. This was the last time that I saw him, since I did not attend the burial.

Since his death, I have never had a dream with him. I wished every night that I would but I wanted to see him alive and talk to him. Fifteen years after his death, I begin to have dreams with him, but they're not how I want them to be. Each dream is like reliving my father's death and I become afraid and want to leave from my dream because it feels so real. Apparently the only way to get out of the dream is to scream my lungs out. My mother told me that the first time it took me ten minutes of screaming to finally wake up, but she had to shake me. Each time, it became worst; it took longer for me to wake up. Tonight my mother had been shaking me with all her force for more than thirty minutes and seeing that I was not waking up she had no other option than to put freezing cold water on me.

My body was shaking and I was still sobbing and breathing hard. "Are you ok sweetie?" my mother asked concerned.

I shook my head, my body trembling. "No, mommy. He's gone, he's gone, he's gone," I whispered.

Through my blurry vision I saw my father leave out of my room. I felt really bad, I hadn't meant to offend him or hurt him. I loved him so much, which was why I called him daddy, but inside I knew that no one would never take my real father's place. I missed him. I did not understand why, but I missed him now more than ever. I shut my eyes, trying to figure this out.

When I opened my eyes, I saw that my dad was back; he held a cup of water in one hand and a Tylenol in the other. He held them out to me with a smile, meaning that he understood me, which I was grateful of. "Here honey. This is going to help you calm yourself and relax."

My mother let go of her arms around me and watched as I took the Tylenol with some hope in her eyes. "Do you want me to sleep with you?" she asked.

"No. I'll be fine. You need to get your own sleep, don't worry about me."

She took the cup from my hands when I was finished and handed me a change of clothes so that I could remove my soaked clothes. She gave me a warm kiss on my forehead before she left, and my dad did the same. "Try to relax honey," he told me before exiting my room, shutting the door in his way.

After changing, I went back to bed, shut off the lights but turned on my lamp. I sat up on my bed, rested my head in my knees, and cried. I cried until I had no more tears and finally closed my eyes hoping not to dream.

"What happened Kaitlin?" Ryan asked with a worried expression when he saw my face, his piercing blue eyes focused on my face as I got in his car.

"Again, again, freaking again!" I yelled in response as I got in and began to cry. He shut the car engine and wrapped me in his arms. I buried my face in his hard chest smelling his cologne as I cried.

"Relax babe. Everything is going to be fine. The dream means nothing. Nothing bad is going to happen to you or your family. I won't let anyone hurt you," he said as he caressed my hair.

I pushed away softly knowing we were going to be late to school of we didn't leave now. I didn't know what I was going to do anymore. I've had the same dream so many times it was driving me crazy and I began to think it was a sign.

"Ahhhhhhhhhhhhh! Help!" was the scream that woke me up. I got up and followed the scream into my parent's room. There I saw my mother holding on the headboard of the bed yelling desperately. I stopped when I saw her feet elevated from the bed, someone was pulling her. My dad was also holding on to her, helping her hold on to the headboard. I ran towards my mother and grabbed on to her trying to add weight. My dad went to fight what seemed like a dark shadow, but he failed. The dark shadow pushed him hard against the wall making him unconscious. I began to cry helplessly as I saw the shadow come closer to me with my mother's feet still in hands. I felt breathing against my face, but I saw nothing. Suddenly, I was lifted up and thrown against the wall leaving me weak.

Through my eyes I saw the dark figure disappear and my mother got up slowly. She walked towards where my dad lay unconsciously, lifted up his head, and after that all I heard was a cracking noise. I wanted to shout out loud, but something was preventing me. My mother walked toward my direction. She stood in front of me. I looked up and dark red eyes staring back at me and a smile. Without saying anything, my mother walked out the room. I urged myself to follow, but I was afraid. The last things I heard were the sound of footsteps and then a door opened and shut close.

"NO. NO. NO!" I screamed after what appeared to be hours of lying on the floor, helpless. "This is a dream. This is another nightmare! I have to wake up, NOW!"

Immediately I ran out of my parents' room, still screaming and rushed into my brother's room. He lay sleeping like an angel. I lay down beside him quietly, my body shaking unstoppably. I closed my eyes hoping that when I opened them again I would wake up from my nightmare.

When I opened my eyes again, I was still in my brother's room and he still lay asleep, breathing at a steady pace. Scared to go back into my parent's room, I got up and forced my feet to walk toward their room.

As soon I stepped into the room, I dropped to the floor and like I had in my dream, I yelled, " Why?!" to the air as I began desperately crying not knowing what to do. I stared at the bed, the bed sheets and pillows were covered with red hand prints. Across the room lay my dad. I focused on him and saw his neck cracked, he was dead. My mother was gone. The only thing I could think of doing at the time was running away. I had to get as far away as possible. I ran out of the room still weeping and went to get my brother.

I didn't know exactly where my strength came from but I wrapped my brother in his blanket and carried him speeding out the house with my cell phone in hand. I ran, not knowing exactly where I was headed. All I knew is that I had to get as far away as I could. A small branch was what finally stopped me. I tripped and luckily the grass by the sidewalk broke my brothers and my fall. My brother was still asleep, and I finally got into some sense and called the police.

"911 what's your emergency?" a voiced asked. I couldn't find the words to explain, all I let out were wimps and sobs.

"Hello? Can you hear me?"

"Yes." That was the only thing I managed to say before falling into tears again.

"Sweetie please relax and tell me what happened. Why are you crying? In order to help you I need you to tell me what happened and where you are."

"It's too late. You can't help now. It's too late, their gone," I whispered in a dead voice.

"Who's gone? Please tell me where you are now."

"Someone or something killed my father, he's dead, and my mother is gone. Please I need help I want to get out of here. I'm scared."

"Oh my God, ok tell me where you are. Give me your name and address. Is there anyone with you?"

"My name is Kaitlin. I live in 356 North Boulevard. I'm with my six year old brother, please hurry," I begged.

"Someone will be there in less than five minutes. Please stay where you are and remain calm," the operator said before she hung up.

"What's wrong Kait? What happened? "

I jumped up startled. My brother had woken up and had apparently heard my conversation with the operator. "Where's Mommy? Is Daddy dead? Kait please answer me," he said before braking into tears and falling into my arms, squeezing me.

I couldn't answer. How was I supposed to tell a six year old that his father was dead and that his mother had killed him and was now missing? It was because of him that I ran out the house. I didn't want him to have to see what I had when I woke up. "Kait, you won't leave me right?" he mumbled through my chest, his breathing uneven.

It was these words that gave me strength. They gave me strength to stop crying and get myself up. I had to keep my life moving because of my brother, he needed me now more than ever. "Listen baby, everything is going to be fine. I will never leave you. Even when I die I will be guarding you, like daddy may be doing right now. I'm going to take care of you and I won't let anyone ever hurt you my love," I said as I patted my brother's head.

He looked up at me. " I'm scared Kait. I don't want to stay by myself. You're the only person I have. I don't want to be alone."

I cupped his face in my hands and wiped his tears softly. "You will never be alone Daniel. Never."

He reached up. With his small finger, he cleaned my own tears, got up, and helped me up. I took his hand and began walking back home. I hadn't run far, only a block.

As I neared my house I saw the police and ambulance there already. A policeman ran toward me and asked, "Are you Kaitlin?"

I nodded. "Are you or your brother hurt?" he asked.

"No."

"Come with me," he said and led us to a cop car, opening the door.

I helped my brother in and I slid in next to him. The policeman said kindly, "I need to take you to the station because we need you to answer some questions. I know how nervous you must be right now, so I'm not going to ask any questions, ok?"

When we finally arrived to the station, a woman approached the car. "Hi guys," she waved through the drivers window," Kaitlin, sweetie, I am going to need you to get out of the car alone so I can question you. I'm sorry, I know you may not want to talk about it right now, but this is a very serious case and we need to start investigating as soon as possible."

I opened the door and as I got out my brother gripped my arm. "Its ok baby, I'll be back. The policeman will take care of you. Nothing bad could happen here," I explained to calm him.

As soon as I got out the woman led me into a black Nissan, I figured it was her car, and that she was a detective. Once we were both inside, she began to speak again, "Hi Kaitlin, I'm Detective Emily, and I'm in charge of you case. I need you to tell me everything about yourself, your mother, your father, you friends, and other family members. But first I need you to tell me the relationship between your mother and father, and what you saw. "

I knew what that last sentence meant. It meant she thought my mother had killed my stepfather. I cleared things up for her. I told her my mother and father had a great relationship. They never fought and never threatened each other. My mother was not the one that had killed my father; it was not her, it was the dark shadow. She was possessed. I told her everything that happened.

"Now are you sure it was not a person you saw pulling your mother? Are you sure it was not your mother that killed your father? Maybe you were hallucinating when you were thrown against the wall and thought you saw red eyes," she asked.

I told her I was sure. It could not have been a person who tried to pull my mother up from the bed because we had no family members or enemies here in Virginia. Our family lived either in other states or in Ecuador. The only people that could be considered family were my boyfriend and my best friend. I described the relationship they had with my parents.

Ryan loved my parents and they loved him. There was nothing more to say. Kathy, my best friend, was basically my parents other daughter. She was like my sister. She slept over my house nearly everyday and she called my parents mom and dad. I didn't know anyone who may try to plot against my parents.

It took nearly two months for my brother's and my life to go back to being somewhat normal. The investigation was still in process and so far no clues were found. My mother was still missing, or as the police said, possibly dead by now. I stopped having the dreams. It was because I had lived what my father had warned me about. Yet, I wasn't sure that this nightmare was over, I felt as though someone followed me.

I moved in with Kathy. Her parents were granted custody of my brother and me. My brother luckily was not traumatized, for he had seen nothing. He cried almost every night though, because he said that he missed Mommy and Daddy. I took care of him and he never left my sight other than when he went school. He was the only piece of family left, and I was not going to let that change. I thought I had him protected, and that whatever that dark shadow was, was gone. I was wrong.

"Don't be stupid and think I've forgotten about you. This is not over. He's next, and there's nothing you or anyone can do about it," read the paper I found under my brother's pillow as I fixed his bed. I tried to understand how. How did the someone or something get in the house and put this here? The only people that lived here were Kathy, her parents, and her baby brothers. One of us would have heard something. My fear began again. I feared not for my life, but for my brothers, and the innocent family living here. I could no longer put them in risk. There was only one thing left to do: run away. I had no other choice.

"Bye baby, I love you," I whispered as I bent down to kiss my brother on his forehead as he slept.

I quietly crept out of the room and left the house. The streets were dimly light and seemed like endless rows of houses. A soft wind pushed the trees in its way. All houses were dark, none lit, as if abandoned. I chose the pathway that led to the park and walked endlessly.

I didn't know why, but I had the feeling that what this thing, whatever it was, really wanted was me. That thing wanted to make me suffer. It was by now obvious that it was following me. It had me under control.

Suddenly, I was blinded and my arms were put behind my back and tied. I didn't scream or kick. This was what I had been waiting for, and I was prepared. My body was lifted and a few seconds later placed inside what felt like a car. The roar of the engine assured me where I was now.

We rode for what seemed like hours. No one said a word, and from the breathing I knew there was only one person in the car and this had to be what was in my parents' room the day my dad was killed. I began to wonder if I was hallucinating about my mother being possessed. "Why couldn't you just get me and not them? Why don't you just kill me now?" I asked, my voice flat yet harsh.

I waited for an answer but there was no reply. I took a deep breath to calm my anger and desire to lunge at this person or thing with all my strength even though I was tied up. After inhaling the air, I suddenly felt like I belonged here, this car's smell seemed familiar. 'Not now, relax;' I kept repeating to myself, 'this person could lead me to my mother, if she's still alive.'

When the car finally reached an end, the driver got off and opened my side of the door and carried me out. The person walked for a little while before I heard a door open. They stepped inside and shut the door, their steps echoing. They laid me down on a cold bare surface that gave me goose bumps. For more than a minute I did not move or breathe. For once in my life I was afraid of what could happen to me. I felt the murderer's breathe near my neck, he whispered, "If you be a good girl Kaitlin and relax nothing bad will happen anyone."

That moment my mind stopped functioning for a second. For an instance, it was as though I heard someone I knew speak to me, but their voice was covered by a harsh and deep voice. I felt a person's lips against my neck, which verified me it was a human, a man, as he began kissing me and pulling my body closer to his. I was afraid of pushing back because the guy may hurt me and I would have never had the chance of finding out if my mother was still alive. "Since your cooperating, I'll remove your blindfold and tape from your mouth so you could give me some kisses back?" asked the guy as he laughed, amused.

I felt his hands travel to the back of my head and what was covering my mouth and eyes was removed. The instant I opened my eyes, I froze. In front of me was Ryan. "Surprise, surprise, eh babe?" he laughed, his eyes deeply focused on mine.

Never in my life had I felt this afraid of a person. Ryan's eyes were now dark black with a red around them, the same eyes my mother had the night of the incident; they could not even be called dark brown. Was he wearing contacts? He was now smiling at me, not his cocky lopsided smile that I loved, but one that I had never on him before, it was the same way my mother had smiled before she left.

I pushed my head back to catch my breath. "Ryan, I have been waiting for this moment for so long, but I want to enjoy you and feel your soft face. Please let my hands and feet go, I promise I try to run. I want you as much as you want me right now," I whispered in his ear seductively, trying to not make it obvious that I knew this was not Ryan.

Without hesitating he untied my hands and feet. I began to kiss down his neck softly, my breath uneven. When I reached his back midneck, I parted my lips and dug my teeth in with all my strength ripping his skin. He screamed in agony and pain and my mouth traveled toward the other side of his neck and I seeped my teeth through his skin once again. This time he picked me up and threw me against the wall as if I only weighed ten pounds. He got up, his face now red, blood dripping down his down his neck. He walked towards me and now I saw his eyes completely red and filled with anger. "Listen bitch, you are going to pay for that!" he threatened. He reached for my hair and dragged me to another room.

I looked around desperately not knowing what to do. As my eyes wondered, I spotted my mother. She was in a corner, her legs and hands tied together. "Kaitlin!" she screeched as soon as she saw me.

"Mom!" I shouted excitedly tears blurring my vision.

"Not for long," Ryan whispered as he once again picked me up and slammed me against the wall leaving me half conscious. Through my half closed eyes I saw him pick up my mother by her hair. He wrapped one of his arms around her neck and walked towards me smiling. "Now I will answer your question from before. I didn't kill you before because you would not have suffered as much as I you will now. I know your rnother means a lot to you. She is the only one you have left. You have no more daddy, no more stepdad, mommy, and no more Ryan."

Even though I was not fully conscious, his words, "No more Ryan," caught my attention. He lifted my lifted my mother by the head, and I knew how he was going to kill my mom. "No," I begged, barely a whisper. I could not find energy to move. My eyes closed shut and my head went down. Ryan lifted my head up and forced my eyes open.

"You are going to look at this whether you want to or not, and you know what you already saw your dad killed this way so now let's try something different," he explained as he lifted my head up and forced my eyes open.

I saw him pull a knife out of his pockets and press it against my mother's neck. "Oh, this is what your daddy, well your actual one, gets for betraying me. I promised him that I would never rest in peace until I got revenge on him, but since he's not here, I'll get revenge by crushing what he loved most, you. I've been following you for years now waiting for the perfect moment when you would suffer the most."

His words caused anger within me and with all my strength I lunged at him slapping the knife out of his hands. My mother was able to get loose but before she could completely get away he grabbed her and twisted her arm before kicking her to the wall.

I grabbed the knife and did the first thing that occurred to me. I stuck the knife in his chest. He did not scream in pain, instead he burst out laughing," You are not hurting me, you are hurting Ryan." Then he snatched the knife from my hands and pressed it against my neck and stuck it in. I screamed in agony and pain, falling to the floor. I felt like millions of needles were being put through my body. My breath was becoming short and my heart beat slowed.

"Well my job is done now, maybe now I can rest in peace," said Ryan and he fell to the floor next to me. I saw something very light gray, barely visible, lift up from Ryan's body and disappear. I looked at Ryan's face his eyes were closed, but just when I started to accept the worst, his eyes opened. They were light blue once again and he whimpered in pain. "Kait what happened? Are you ok?" he asked softly with a cough and a face, he was in much pain as I was.

"It doesn't matter if I'm fine or not. I'm sorry I stabbed you, I'm sorry," I weeped. It hurt to talk.

He looked at me, and his eyes closed. He made an effort to open them for the last time and say, "I love you."

"I love you too," I replied and my eyes shut. Forever.

What surprises have your received recently?

DIVAS OF THE DEAD

May all my dead divas please rise...

Rise up outta ya grave and show

them skeleton thighs!!

It's a full moon tonight

Let's go out and cause

A terrible fright

Let's find us a funky groove

While dancin' beneath

The pale moonlight, But

Remember my Divas

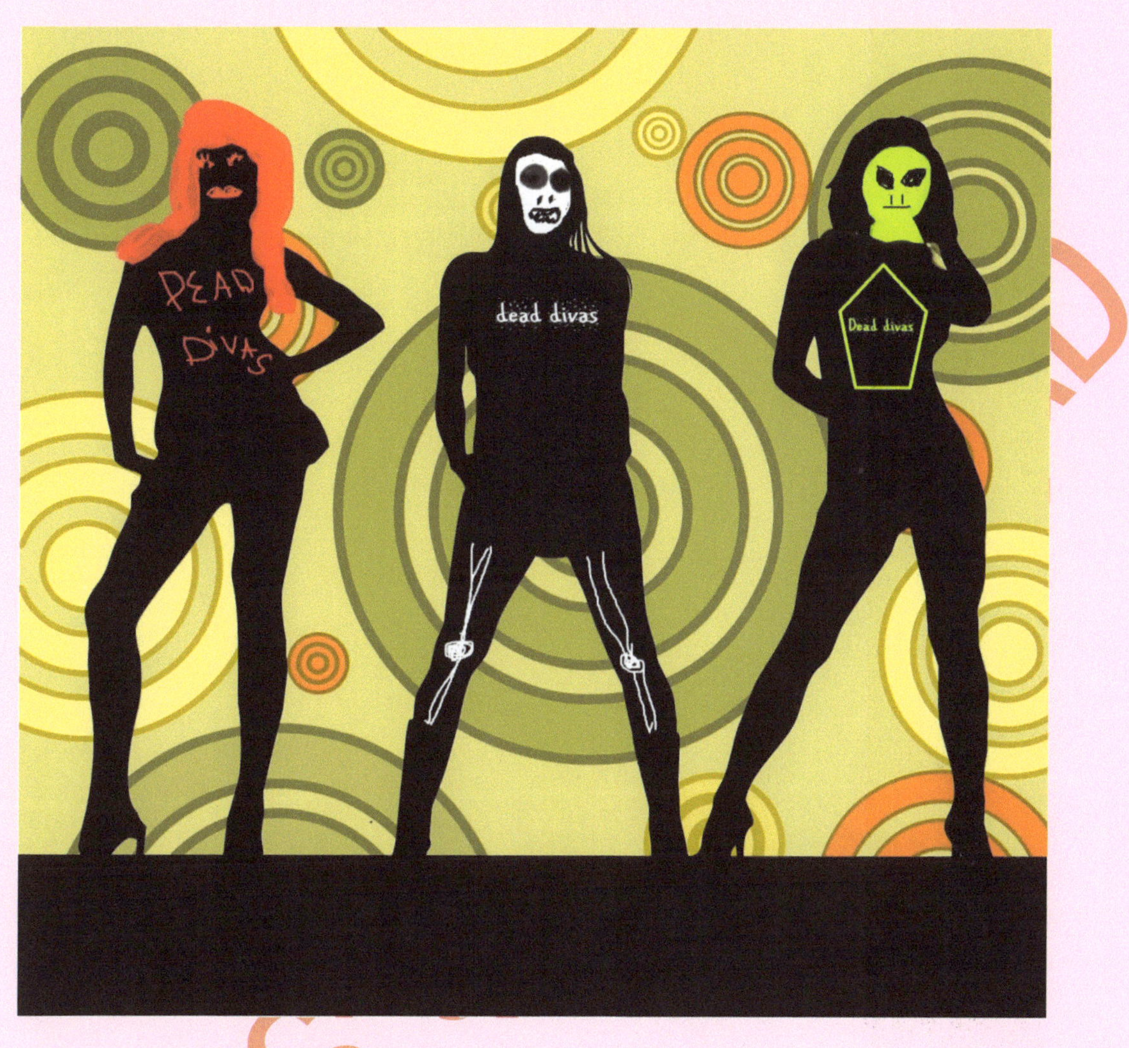

We only got until midnight

-MANIYAH THIGPEN

DIVA THOUGHTS
What divas do you like? Not Like?

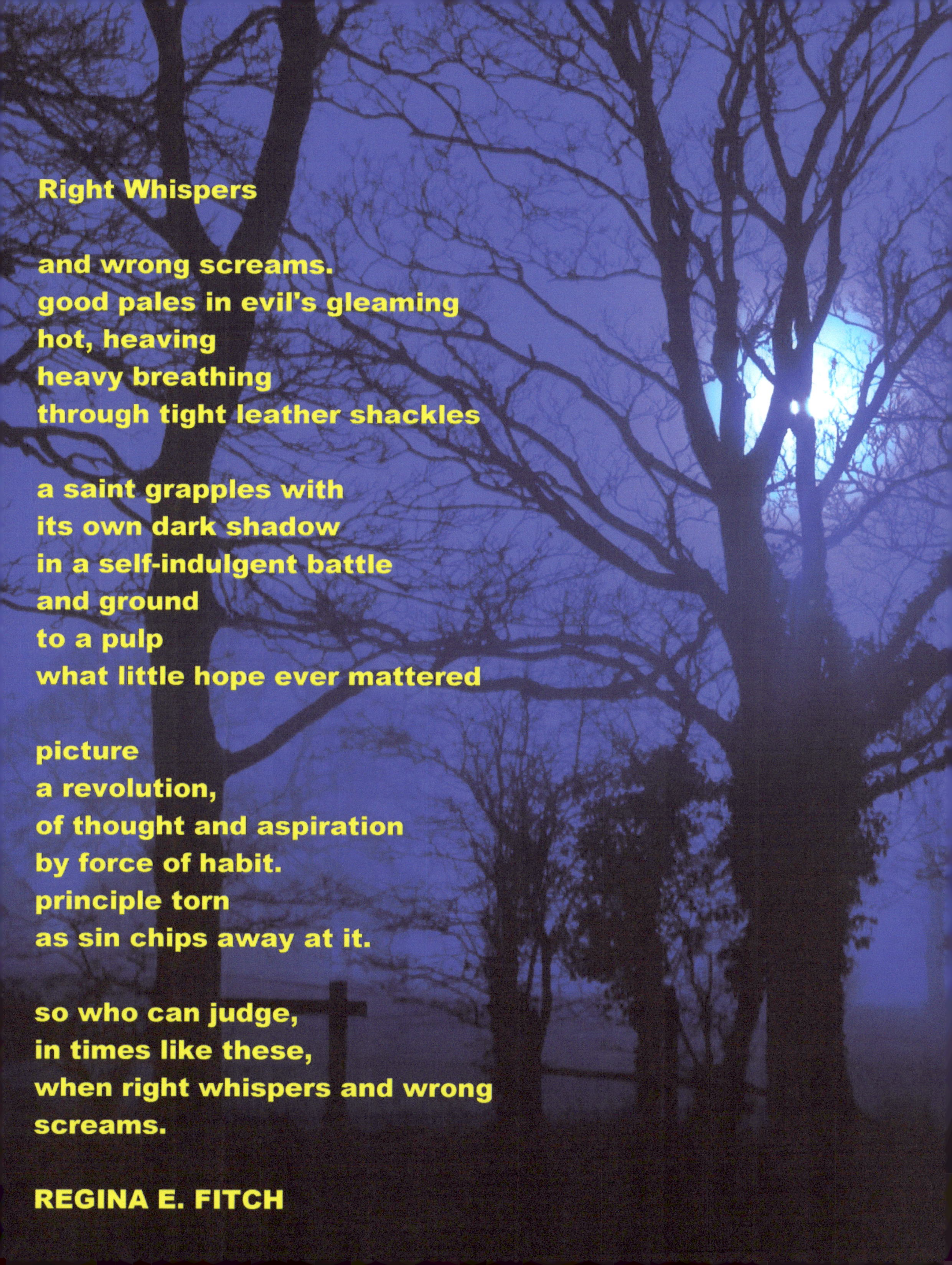

Right Whispers

and wrong screams.
good pales in evil's gleaming
hot, heaving
heavy breathing
through tight leather shackles

a saint grapples with
its own dark shadow
in a self-indulgent battle
and ground
to a pulp
what little hope ever mattered

picture
a revolution,
of thought and aspiration
by force of habit.
principle torn
as sin chips away at it.

so who can judge,
in times like these,
when right whispers and wrong
screams.

REGINA E. FITCH

What do you whisper about in the dark?

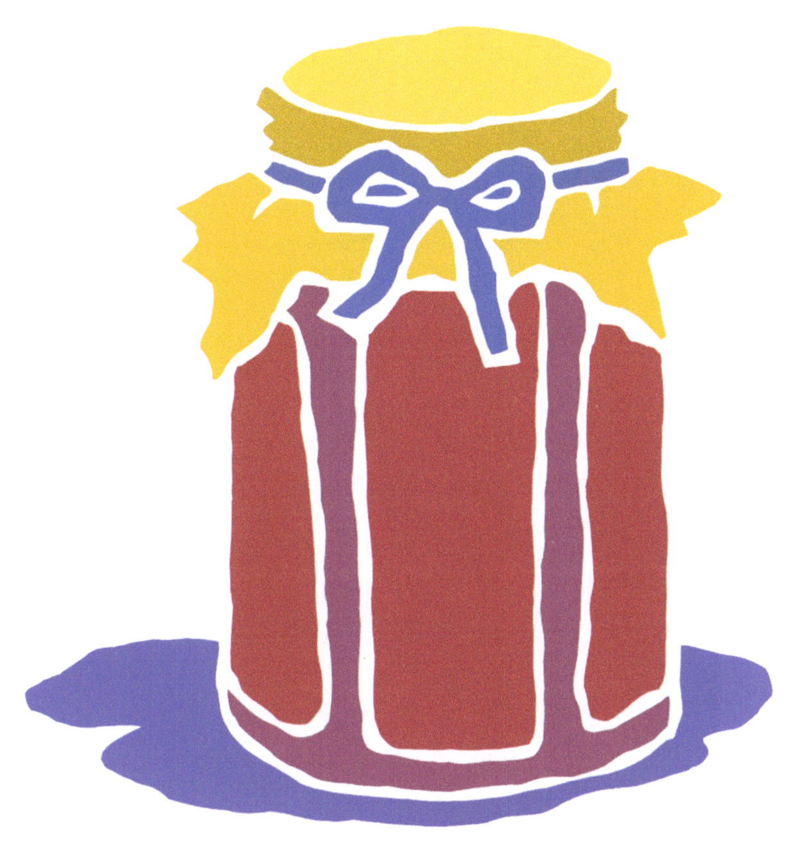

Hi! My name is Jelly…See my Story!

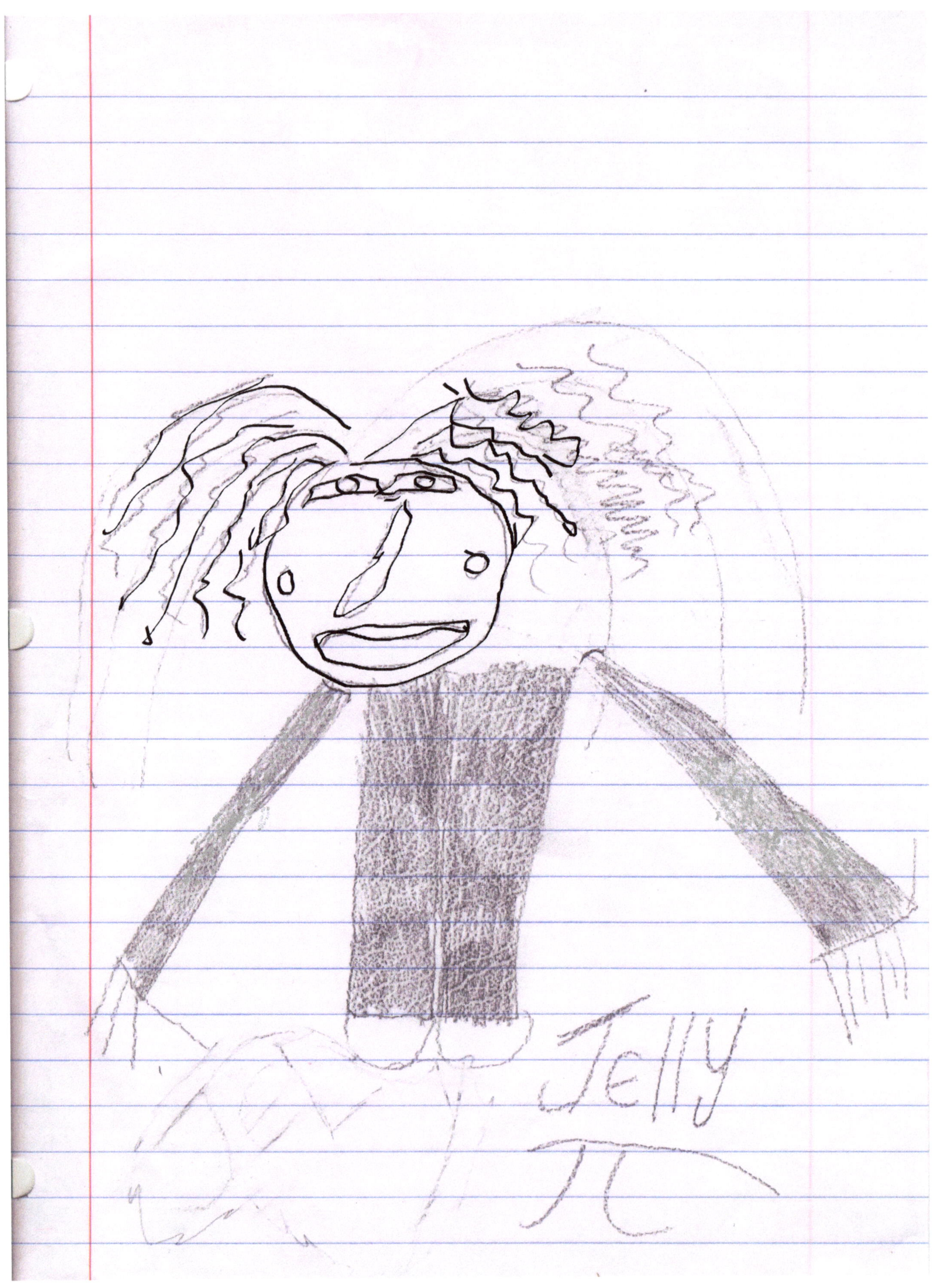
Jelly

Big lil Waim

Has 6 tattoos on his arms, stomach + head.
He has 2 sons and 1 daughter who are not as ugly as him. Although his daughter has his beady eyes of purple His wife thinks he's cute. She loves him for his crazy hair. He lives in a Tree town house and sings an evil song while dancing an evil dance all day long. Keep away from big lil waim because he's bad as he can be.

by Jelly + R.E.F

How do you stay away from evil?

MY DARKNESS

BY

JEFFREY CABAN

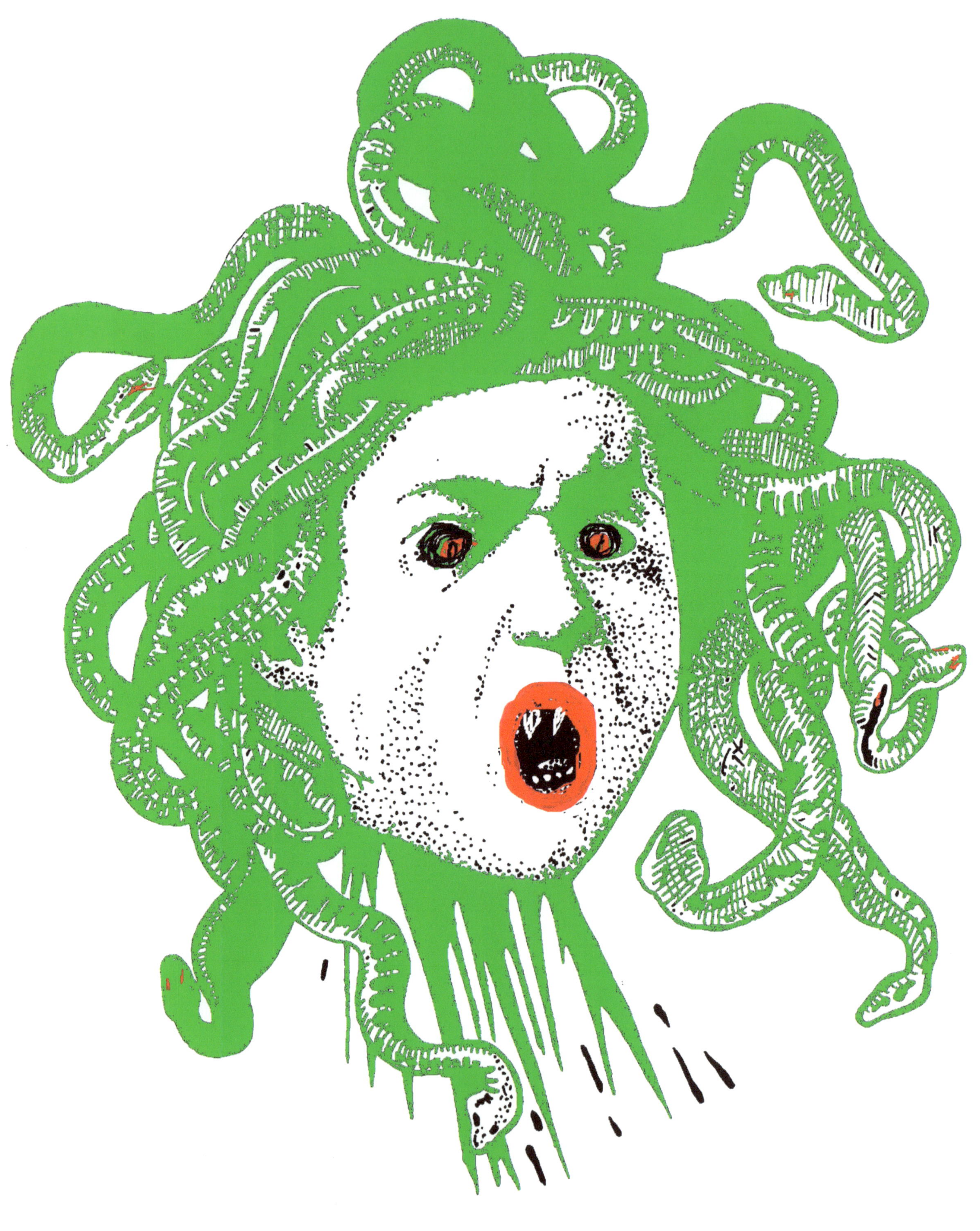

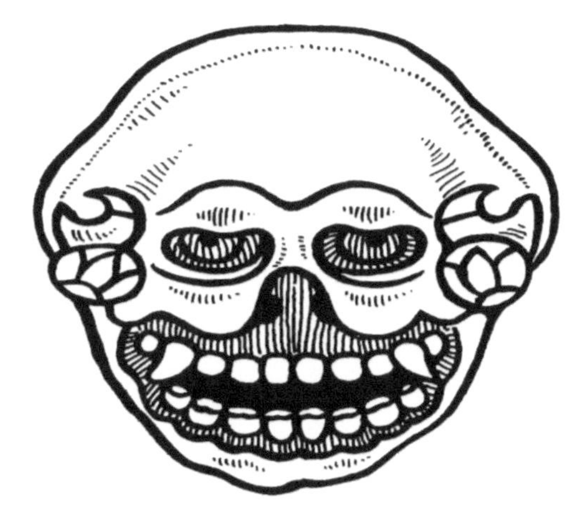

YOU MAY NOT REPAIR MY
SOUL;
WHETHER YOU GIVE ME MONEY OR NOT;
I WILL NOT CARE
BROTHERS
YOU'VE TAKEN FROM ME
CRUSHING MY HEART AND SPIRIT
SEPARATING US
SHE KILLS ME EVERYDAY
'CAUSE SIBLINGS AREN'T LIVING THE LIFE
IT FEELS LIKE I'M BEING STABBED WITH A KNIFE.
SO MOTHER'S LITTLE SISTER

IS SO CALLED LIVING THE PERFECT LIFE

WHILE MY LITTLE BROS,

WEAR CLOTHES

TWO YEARS OLD.

NINETEEN YEARS AGO,

MY COUSIN WAS SOLD;

NOW SHE'S BACK

BUT WE NEVER KNOW

THE TRUTH.

MY DARKNESS

MY FEAR EVERYDAY

IS THAT LIFE IS GOING TO REPEAT ITSELF.

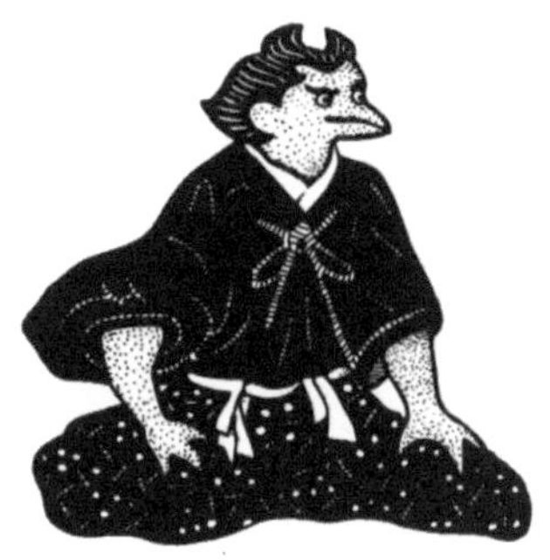

JEFFREY CABAN

What is your darkness?

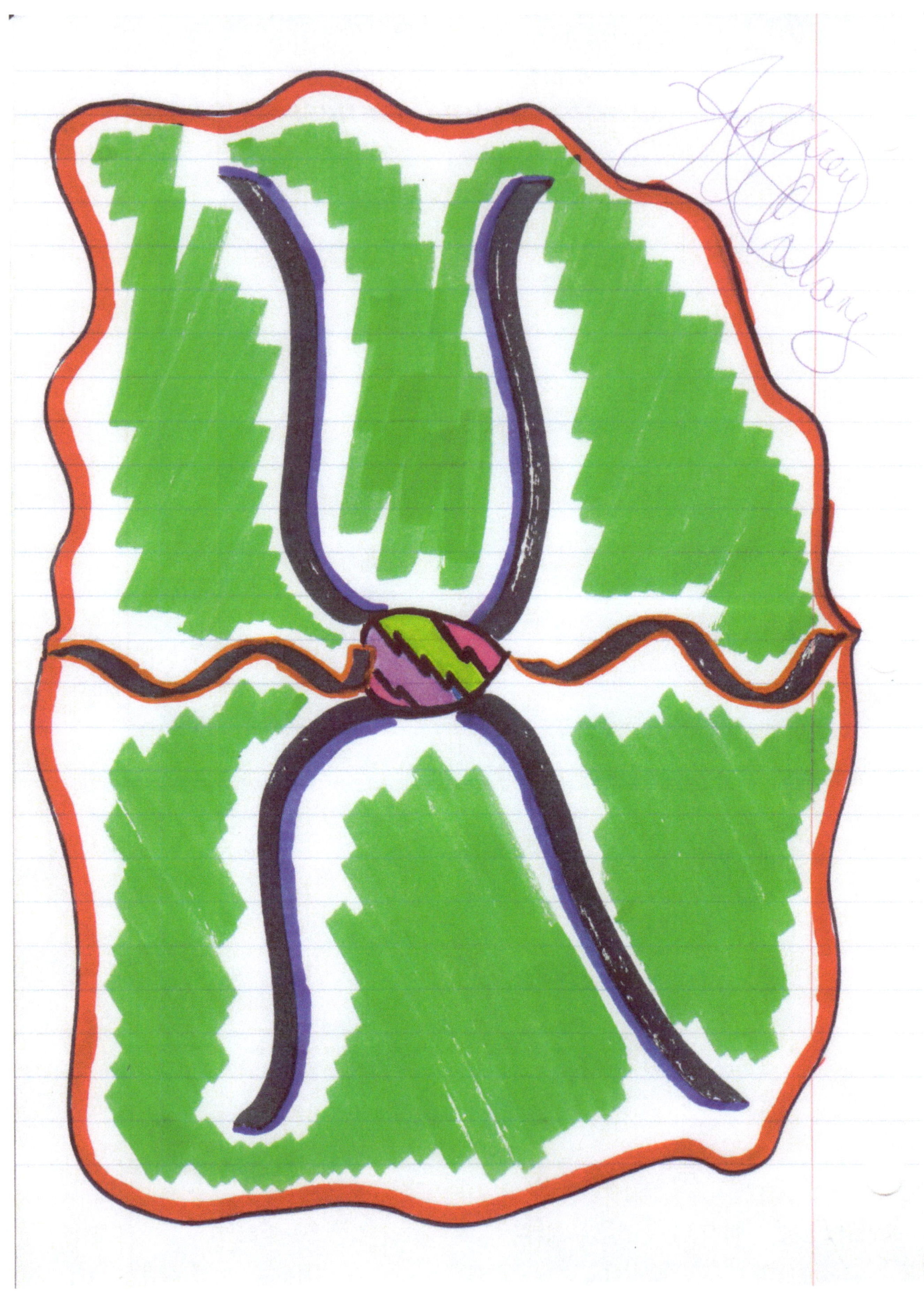

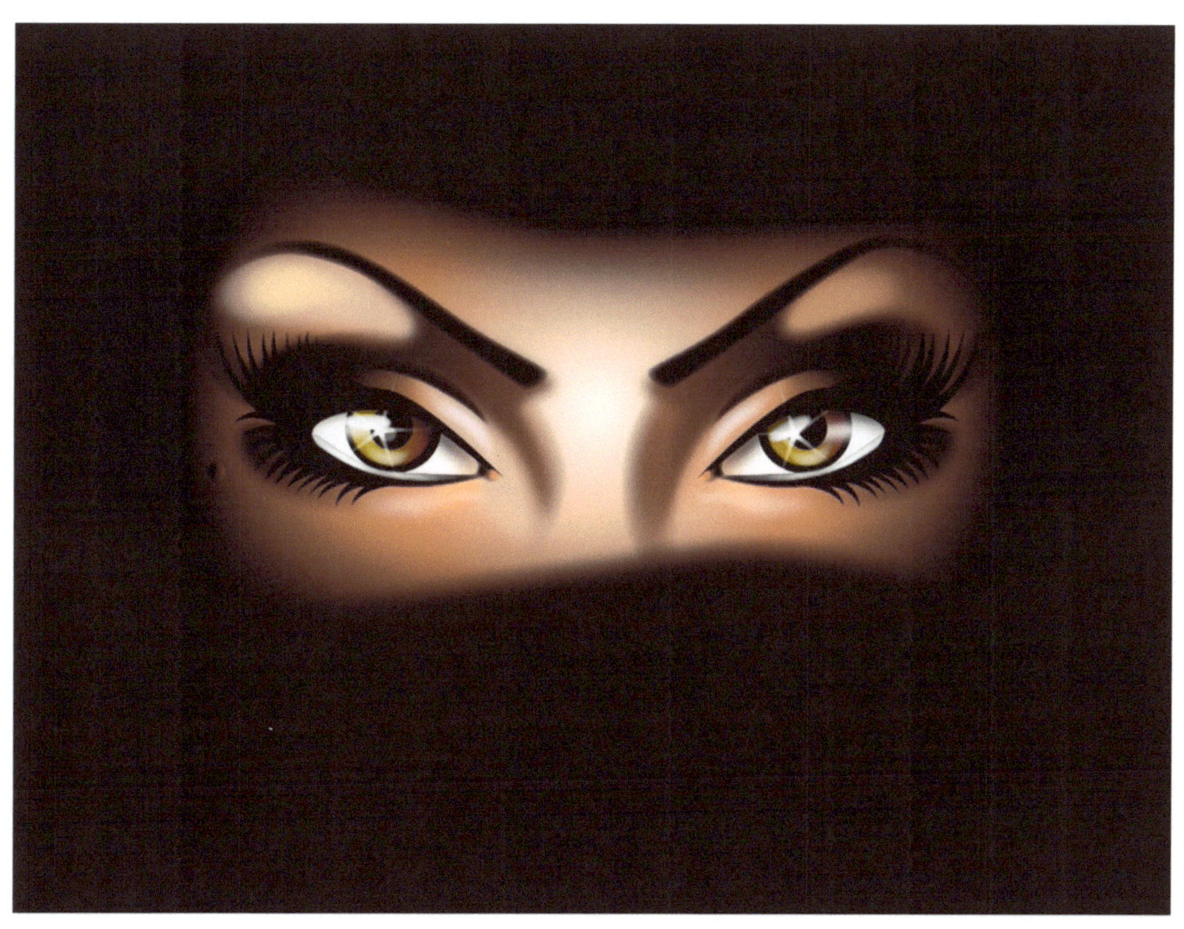

Hey! You want to see my "EYES IN THE NIGHT?"

Just turn to the next page...

by Raquan Frazier

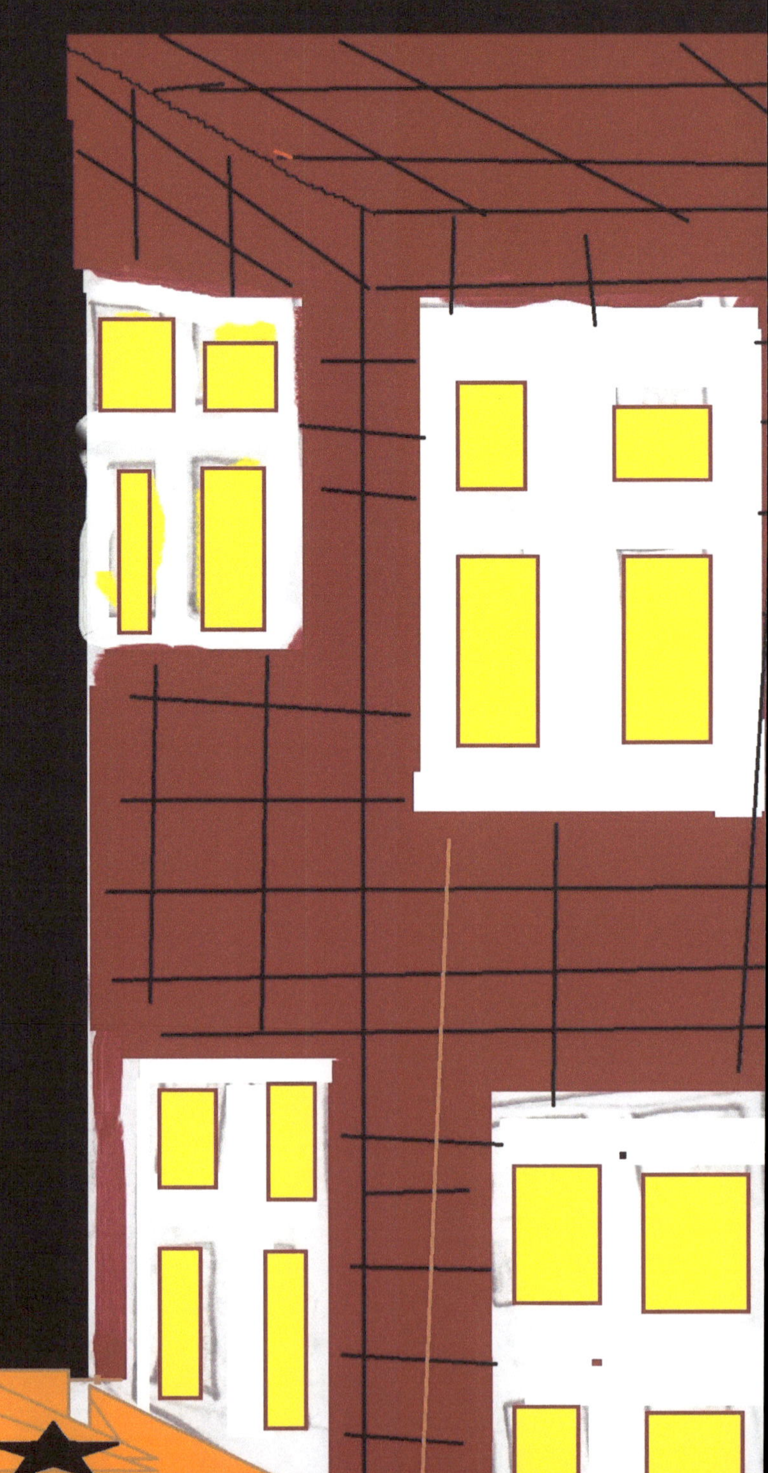

Raquan Frazier

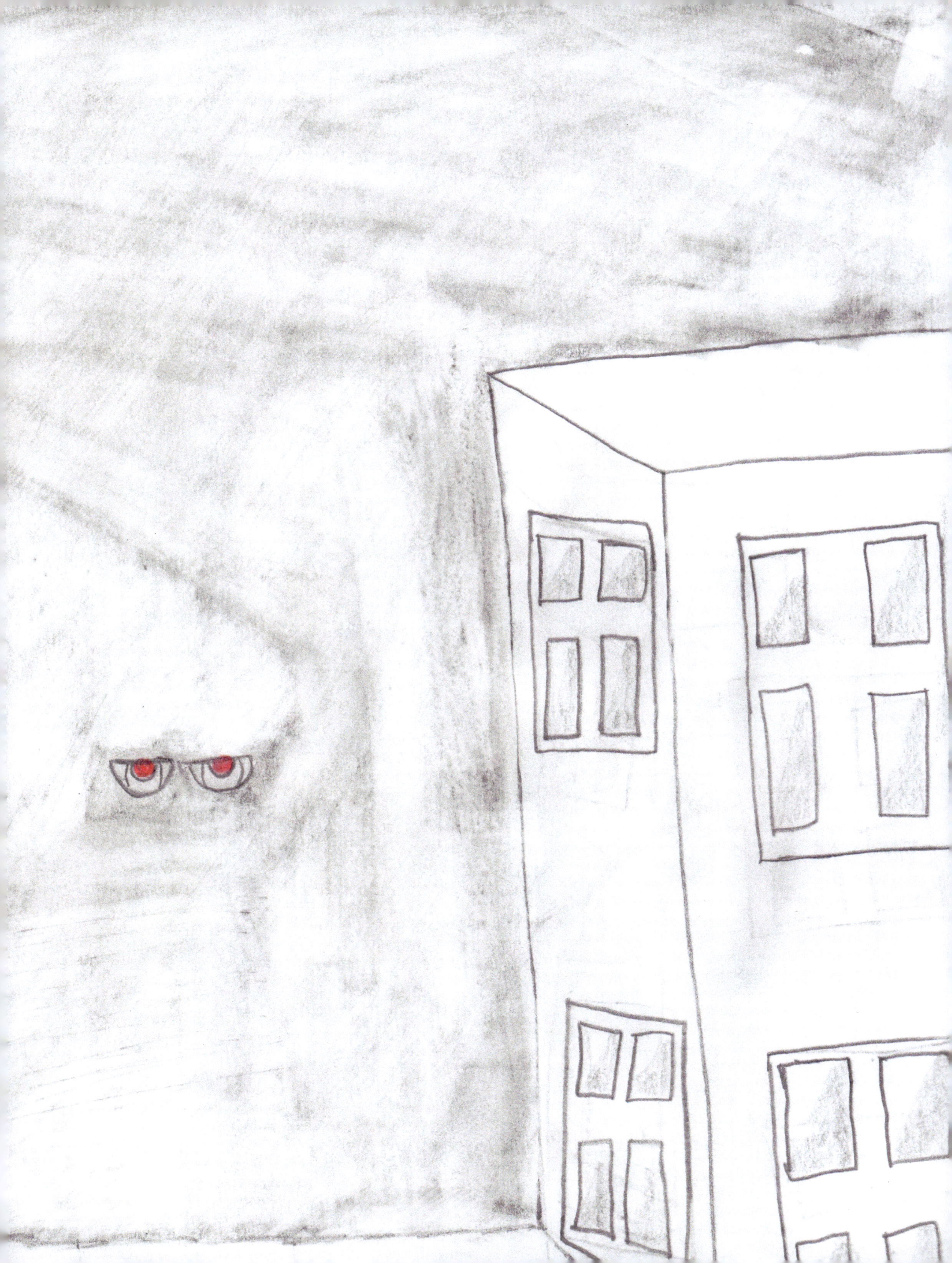

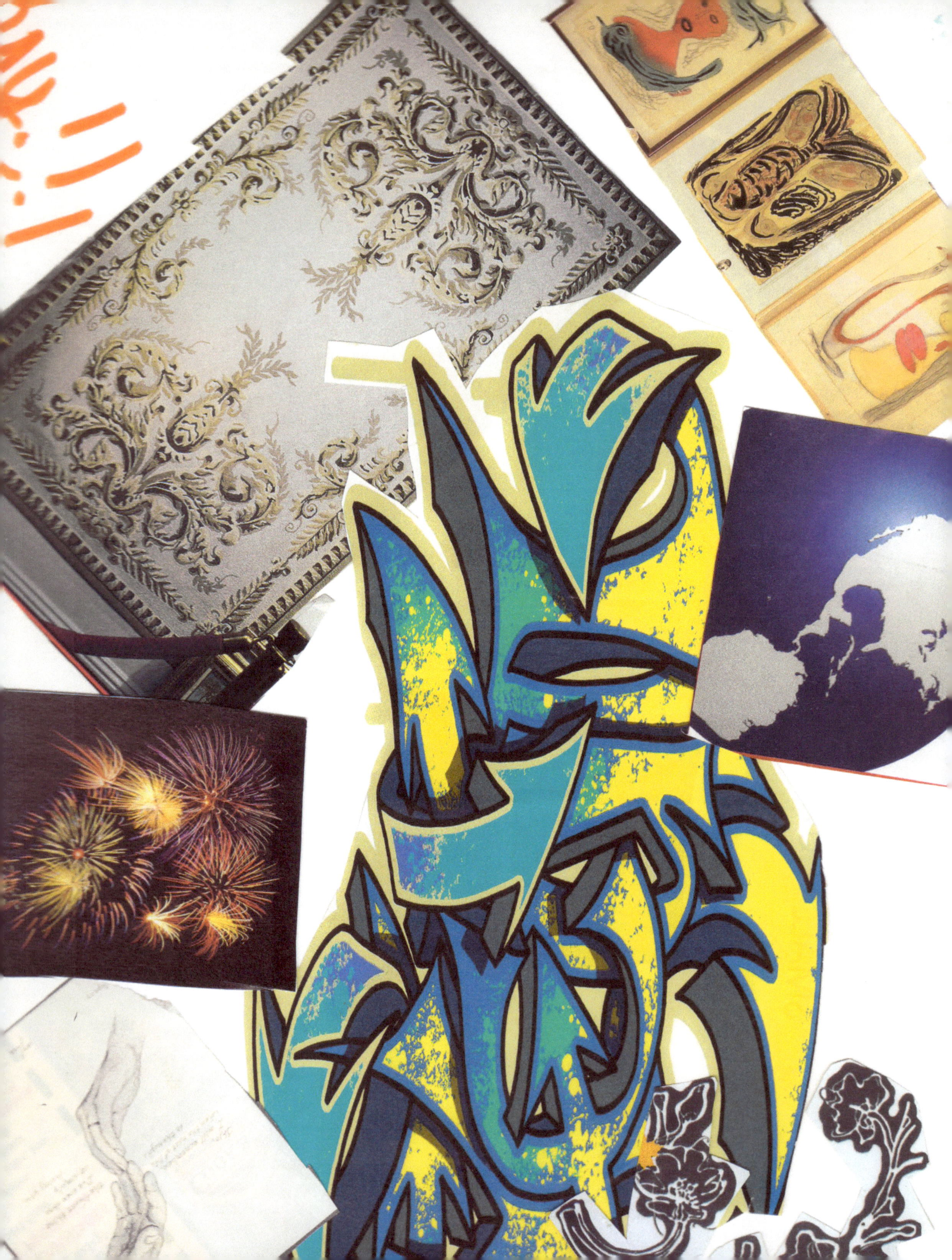

UNDEAD HOLLY MOLLY

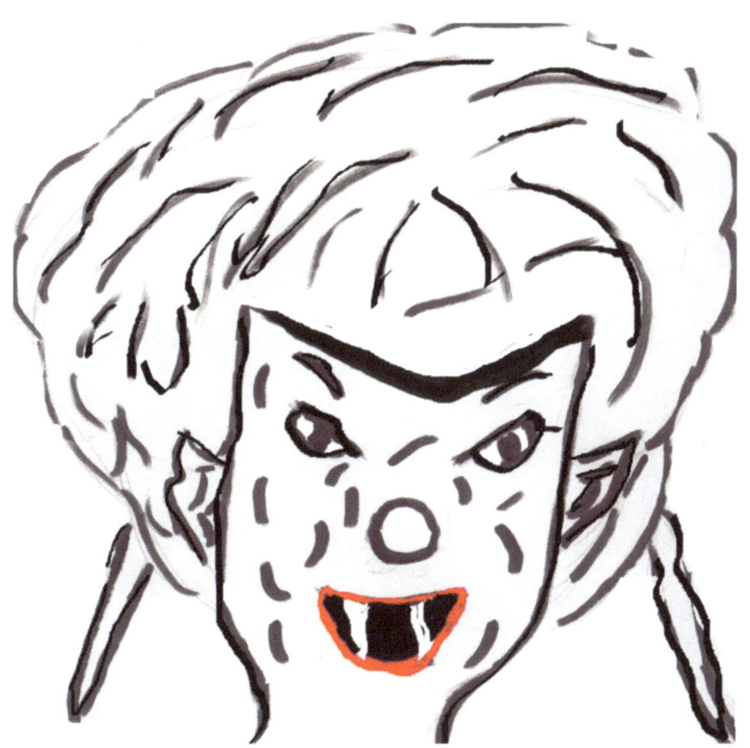

RennettMitchell

2011

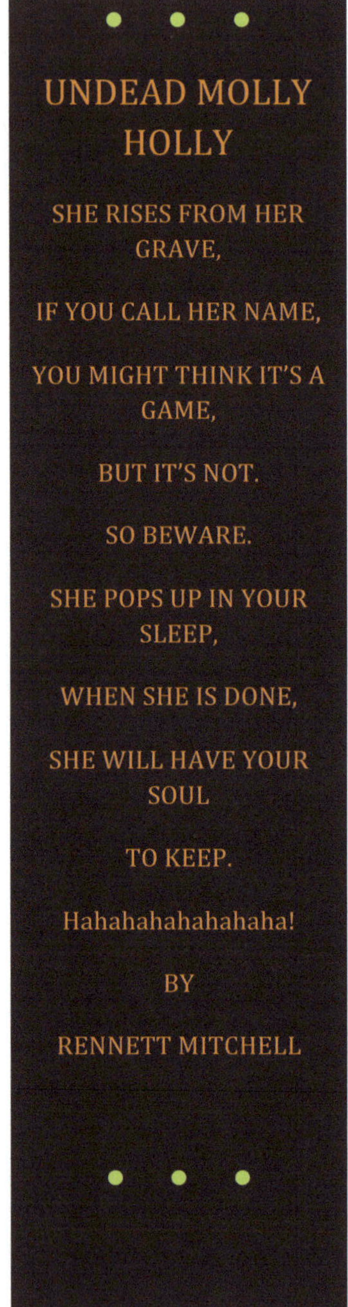

UNDEAD MOLLY HOLLY

SHE RISES FROM HER GRAVE,

IF YOU CALL HER NAME,

YOU MIGHT THINK IT'S A GAME,

BUT IT'S NOT.

SO BEWARE.

SHE POPS UP IN YOUR SLEEP,

WHEN SHE IS DONE,

SHE WILL HAVE YOUR SOUL

TO KEEP.

Hahahahahahahaha!

BY

RENNETT MITCHELL

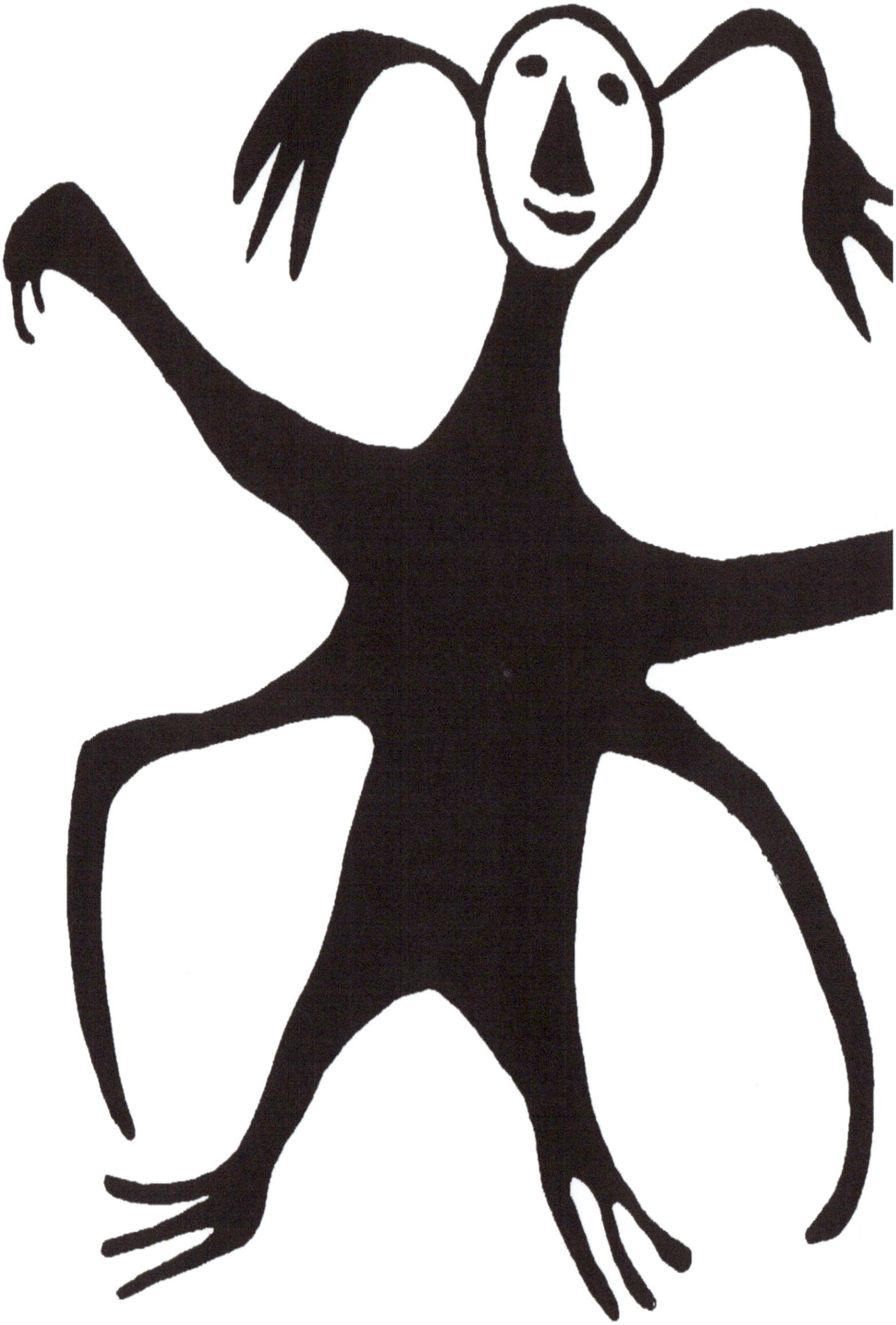

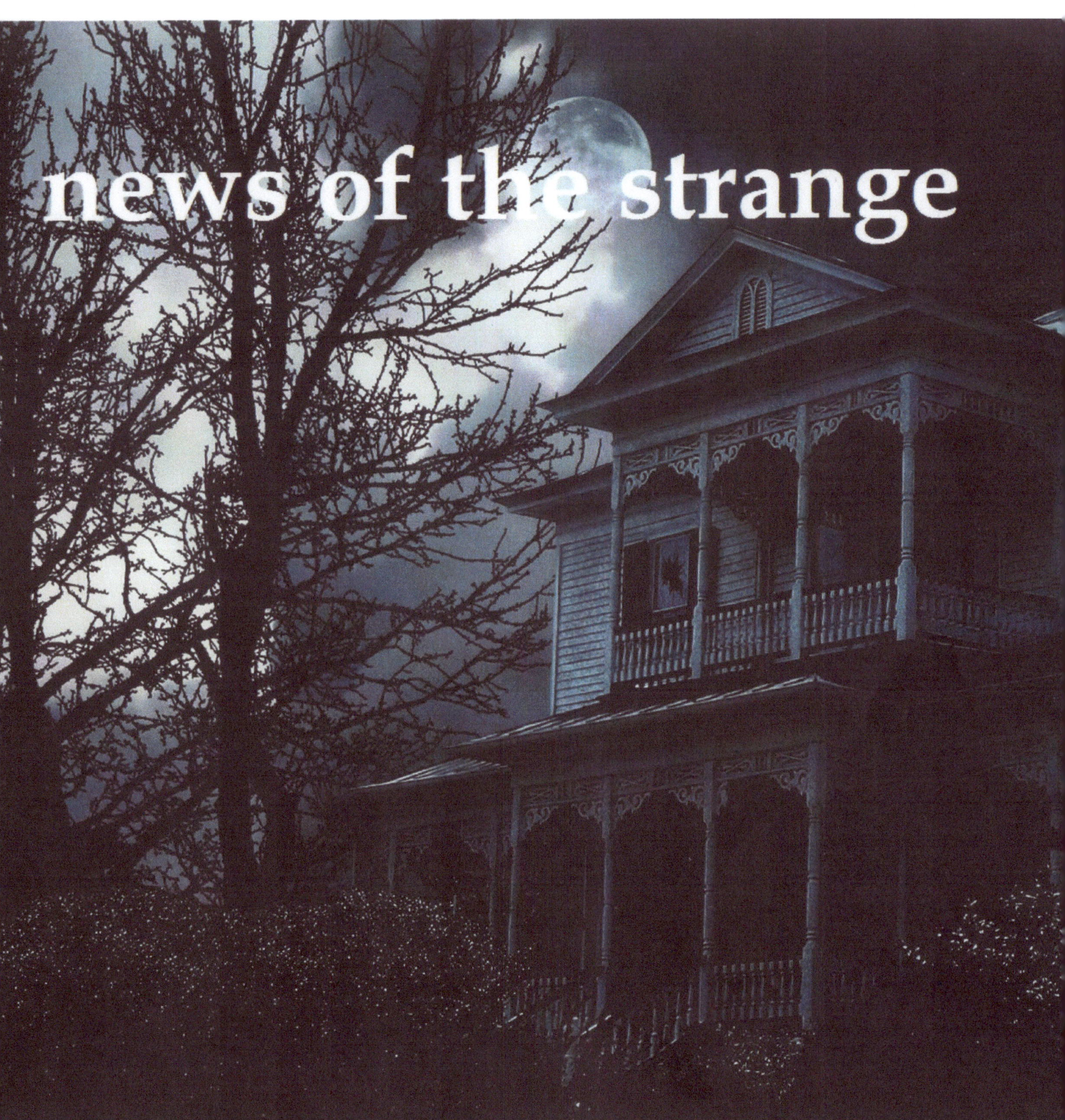
news of the strange

THE THOMPSON TIMES

Evening edition

"All the news, all the time"

REACH YOUR PROSPECTS FIRST

Killer Clown BOLA in Town

Citizens running for their lives

Reporter Emauni Thompson on scene

Newark, NJ- A family moved into a house not knowing that it had been occupied by BOLA, a killer clown. One by one family members have mysteriously disappeared, and the father was found hanging from a bathroom ceiling.

BOLA has a green face consisting of green dripping paint, and eyes that are completely black because he has no soul. The only evidence police on the scene had found was a green clown nose. There are no clues as to his whereabouts.

Keep a sharp eye out for BOLA, the killer clown.

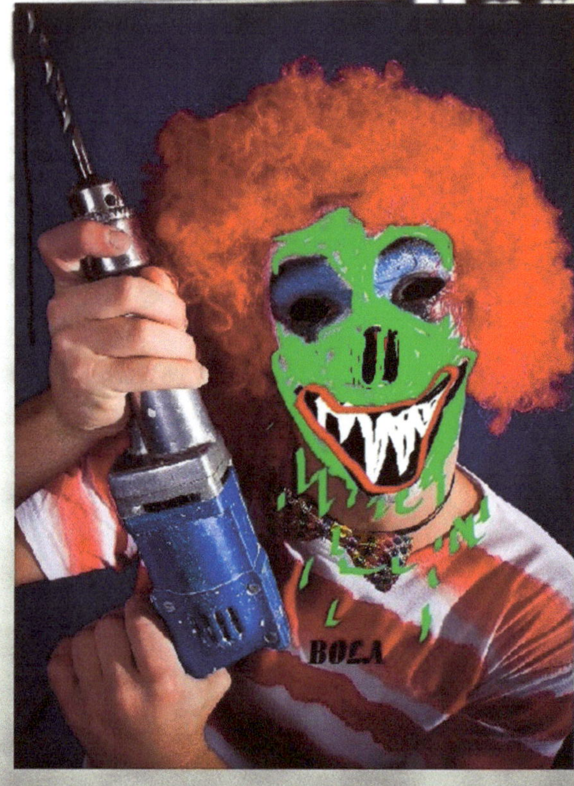

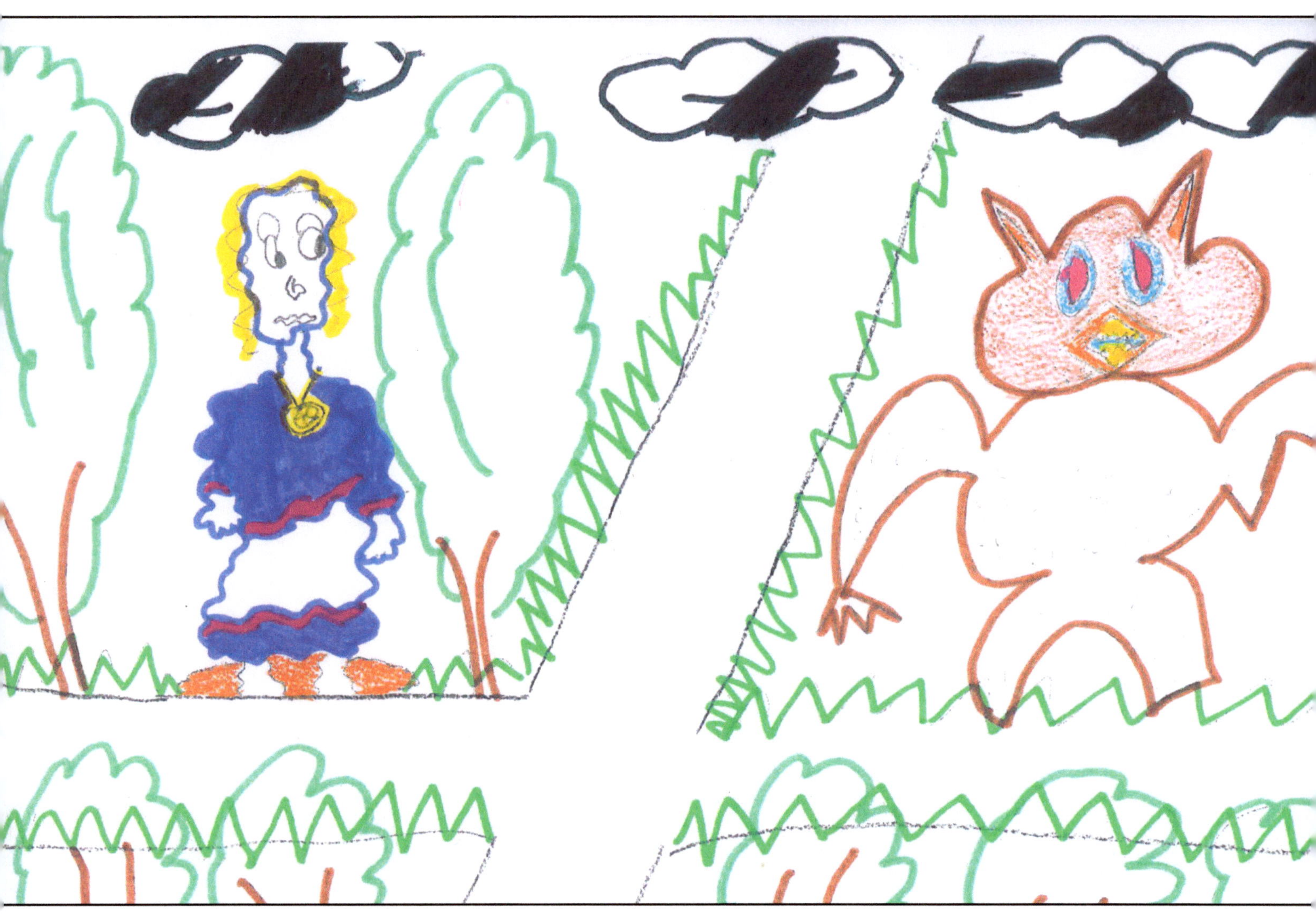

So what strange news do you hear these days?

Whatever Happened to that girl named Lisa?

by

Joshshea Bonds

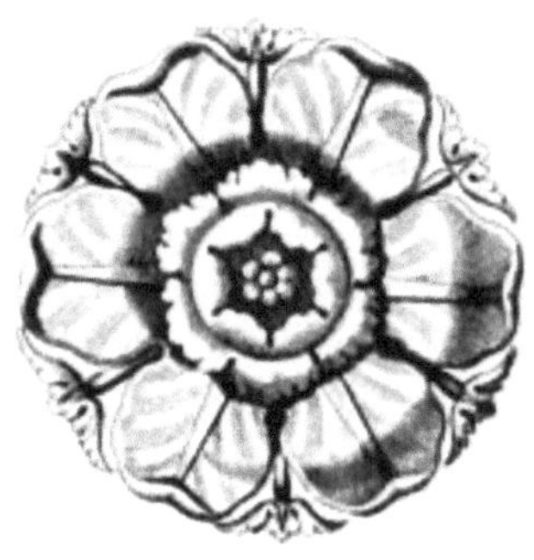

The year was 1958 when everybody danced to their own rhythm, their own beat. If you didn't belong to a clique, you were considered an outsider, and outcast. Jamie McCrow knew this; she was the biggest outcast ever. People called her Witch McCrow because of what she would wear and how she always stood alone.

Jamie's mom passed away when she 13 years old. I am not sure how she died, but the story around here is that Jamie's father killed her mother because she wanted to leave him. He wanted to make sure that Jamie didn't leave him either so he locked Jamie in the basement. He wanted to make sure that she wouldn't leave him either. Her father died leaving her alone...until one day when she decided not to be alone anymore.

It was on a dull, dark, loud, rainy night when my friends and I walked on Shadow Creek Road, and Lisa shouted, "Hey you guys! Let's go into Old McCrow's house."

"No! Didn't you hear of stories of how every person that went into that house never comes out?"

"Don't worry, " she said, "no one is there. Those are just old stories to frighten people.

So we walked up to the stairs and each stair squeaked with a skin crawling sound. With my first look of the building, a sense of fear came over me. My spirit could not settle down, so I said, "Hey you guys, maybe we should just turn around and go to Zack's party?"

"Stop being a punk, Liz. Everything's going to be okay, so come on. We opened the door and walked in the house. The door slammed behind us with a BANG! We all jumped.

Lisa led the way. "Come on Liz, Tammy, let's see what's over here. We walked into what was once the parent's bedroom. Blood spotted the walls and the floor.

"Help! Please help! a voice shouted from the basement.

"Who's there?" Tammy yelled back.

"Please help me! I don't want to be alone anymore someone yelled again from the basement.

I watched as Lisa walked to the basement door,and put her hand on the doorknob to open it.

"Stop!" I yelled. "Don't go down there. It has to be Jamie McCrow, and everyone knows if she calls you and you go, you never come out."

"Oh Liz, those are just rumors." Lisa replied. What if this person really needs our help? What if we leave, and she hurts herself and dies? We will be responsible for it. Let's go."

"No, I don't feel right. I am not going down there. Lisa, don't go."

Lisa looked at me and she looked at Tammy. "Are you coming, Tammy?" she asked softly.

"I don't know, Lisa. Maybe Liz is right. Maybe we should just call the police and they can check it out." Tammy replied.

"I'm going. You guys can stay here if you want. I am going to help her." As Lisa opened the doors a strong wind burst from the basement, sending chills down our backs. That voice coming from the basement whispered, "I am down here. Come on and be with me."

Lisa turned around and looked at us. She started back up the stairs, but the door slammed in her face.

"YOU ARE NOT LEAVING ME!" screamed the voice from the basement.

"Help me! Help me!" Lisa yelled while she banged on the door. Tammy and I couldn't open the door. Then suddenly the banging and yelling stopped.

Tammy and I ran out of the house, yelling and crying, telling everyone what happened. Our parents and the police went to the house. They opened the basement door, and went down into the basement. The police didn't see anyone or anything.

"Girls," a police officer asked," are you sure she was down here? I could tell by the officer's eyes that he didn't believe us. "Maybe she will show up at her house. She might be playing a trick on you guys. So go home and get some rest."

The morning came and passed. The days and weeks passed as well and no Lisa.

Everyone say that she just went away to be with her boyfriend. Other stories would develop, too. But no one would really tell the story of how she disappeared but me.

I knew the truth. 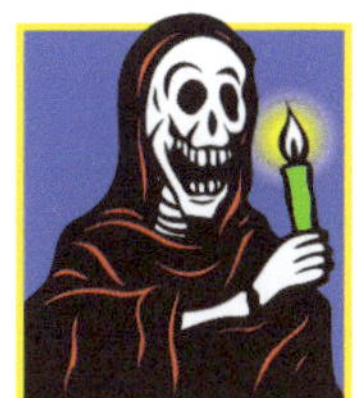

EVERYBODY KNOWS ABOUT THE MONKEY IN THE CLOSET ON THE NETWORK SHOW "FAMILY GUY."

BUT NOBODY KNOWS THAT HE HAD A BROTHER…

DIRTY MONKEY EVIL BACK.

LIKE HIS BROTHER, HE, TOO, LIVES IN THE CLOSET OF A HOUSE. HIS PURPOSE IN LIVE IS TO SCARE PEOPLE AND RIP UP STUFF.

HIS WEAPON OF CHOICE AGAINST PEOPLE IS A BOTTLE OF HOT SAUCE.

THIS IS A HAWKIN'S TRIBUTE TO FAMILY GUY'S MONKEY IN THE CLOSET…MEET DIRTY MONKEY

BY NAJEE HAWKINS

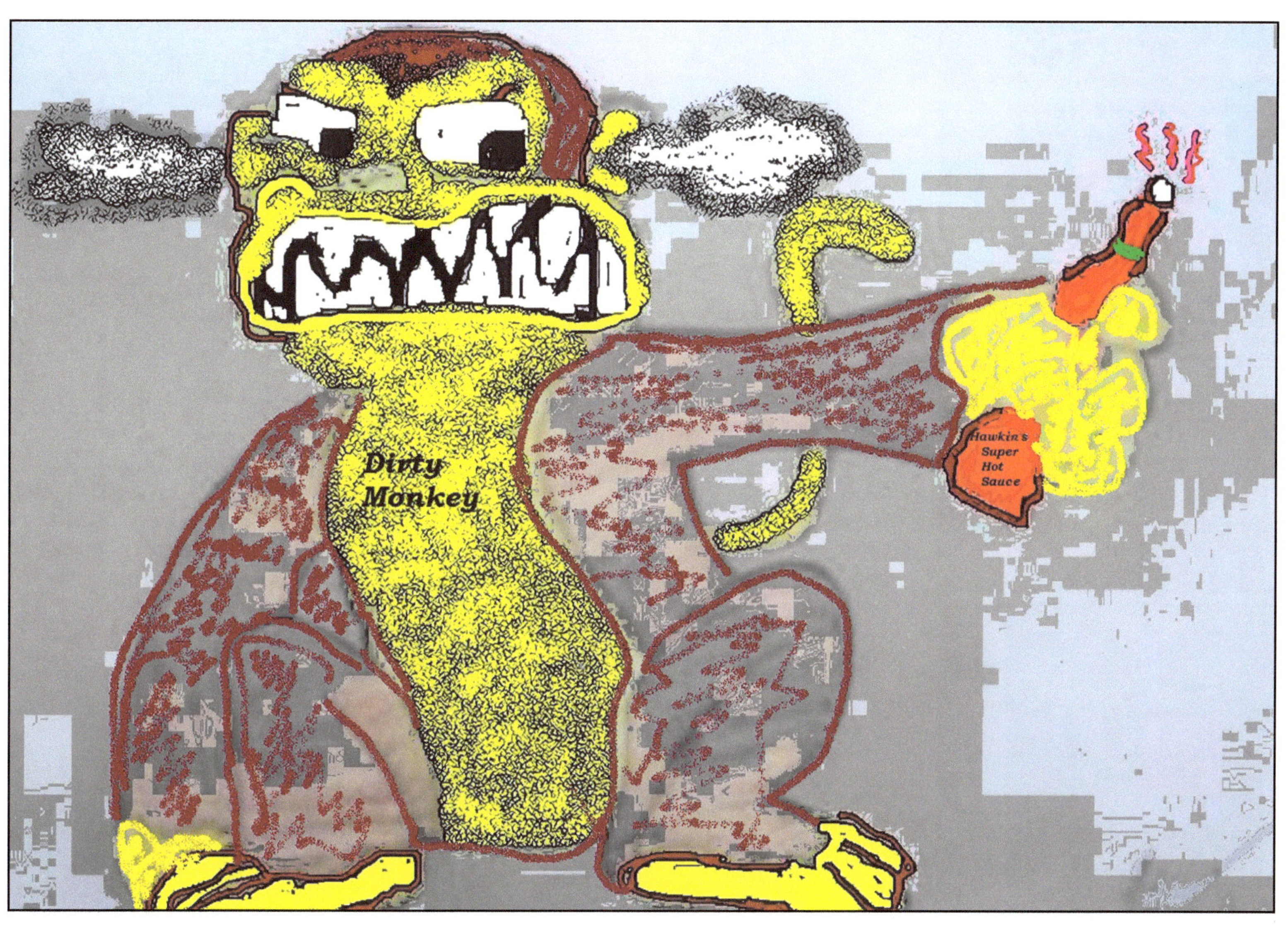
Dirty Monkey
Hawkin's Super Hot Sauce

Have you ever seen a Bad Monkey?

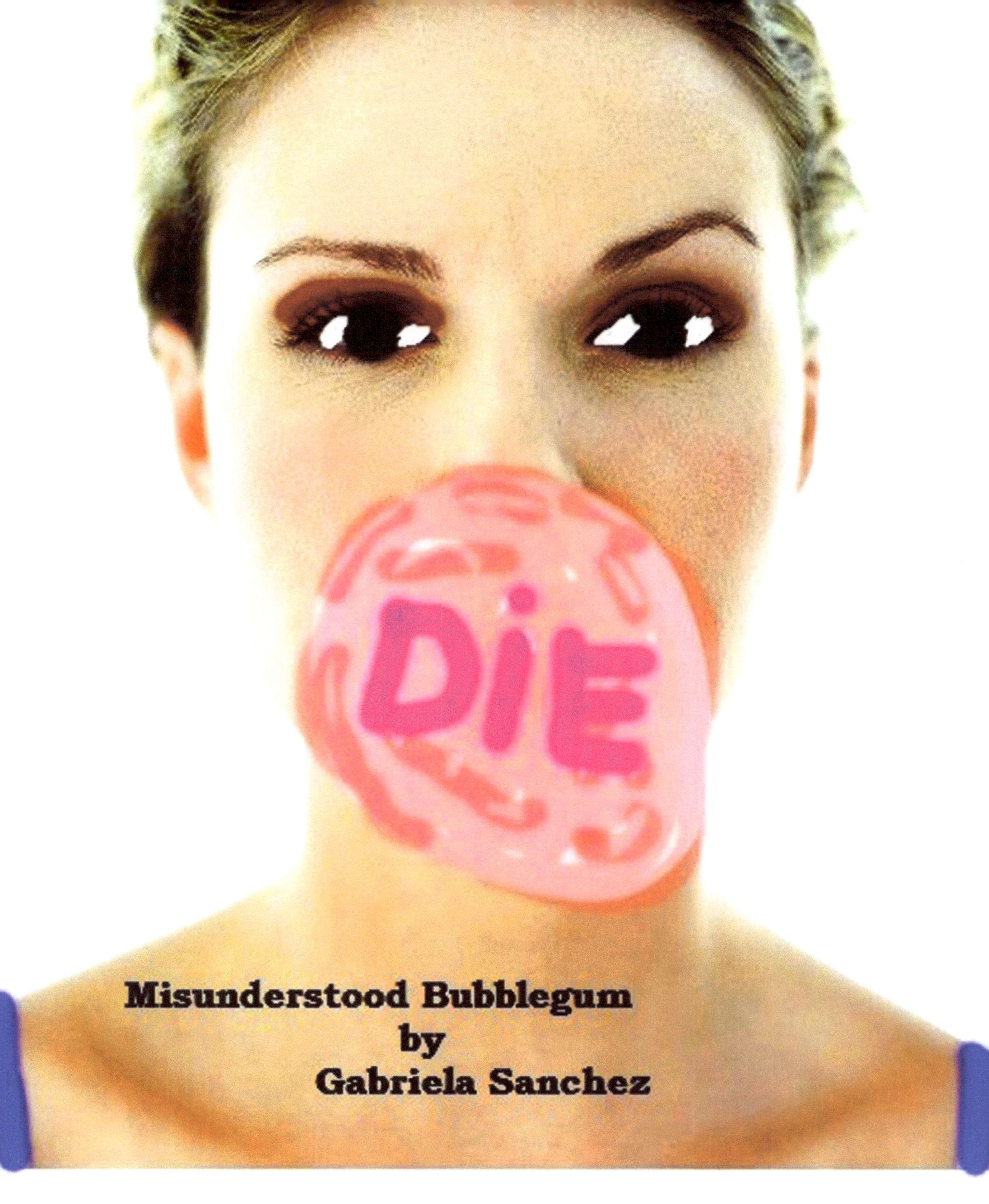
DiE
Misunderstood Bubblegum
by
Gabriela Sanchez

No one understands me as I snap my gum in
class.

The gum I chew relaxes me, it's a feeling I know
that nobody has.

I watched the clock's hands move as I hear time
pass by

but nobody understands the anxiety

that makes me tremble inside.

Life is scary when you don't know what to expect,
so will continue to chew my gum as a
comforting method of the misery I fear I will
face some day.

My friends complain I chew too much gum,
but they simply don't understand
how it is the only way I feel safe on my way
from the cave

they'll never know the truth that I change into
a monster, a scary looking creature

as I walk through the cave, killing every
person that gets in my way.

There is no way of escaping this creepy
cave, because that's my home.

That's where I was born and raised.

I am human in the day but a monster at night
and I wish people would just stay away stop me

from attacking them.

This is why my bubblegum is misunderstood.
I chew it every day, to calm anxiety
from worrying if I'll ever attack anyone during the day.

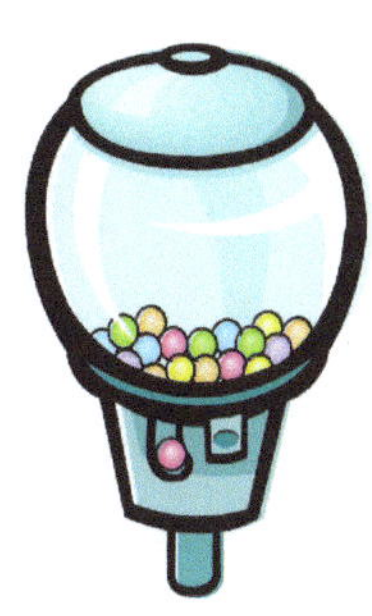

How much gum do you chew?

When there's

quiet in the mad house
silence in the hall
wind between the floorboards
rush, retreat, ensue
soothing
strength of legend

Ghost stories come true
when green eyes turn to brown
and wishful
stops and stares at you.

Regina E. Fitch

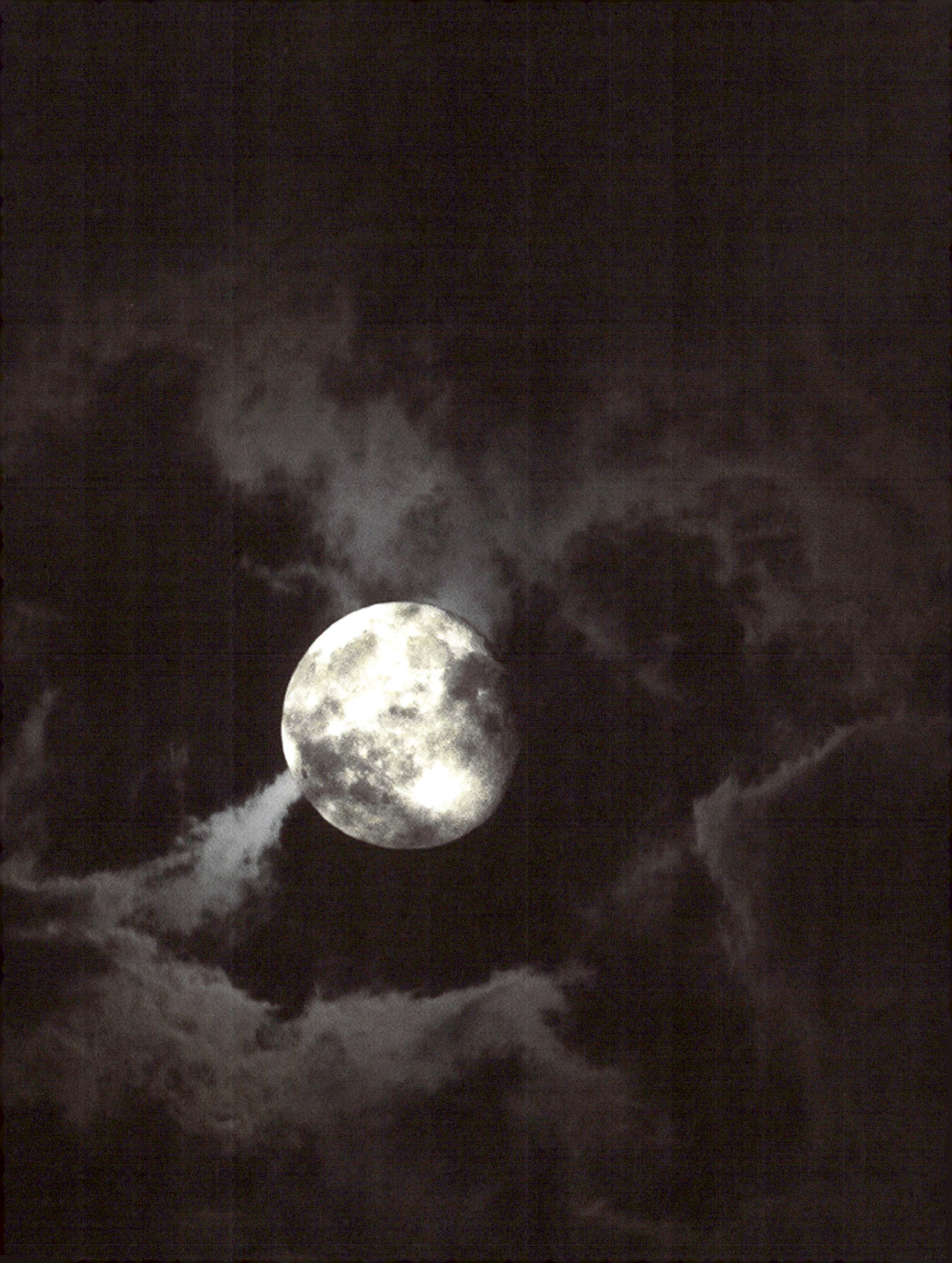

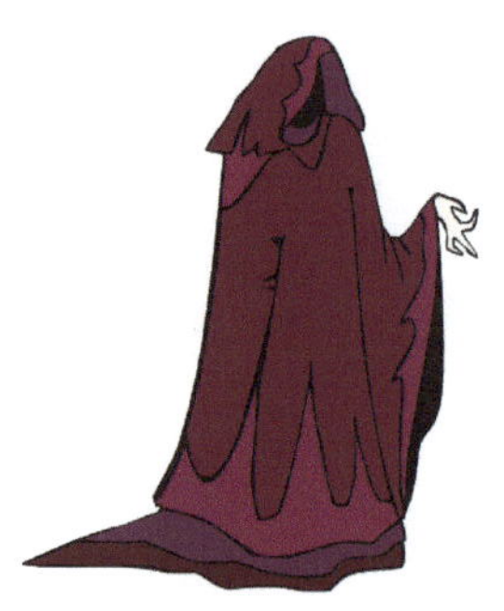

So what ghost stories have you heard lately?

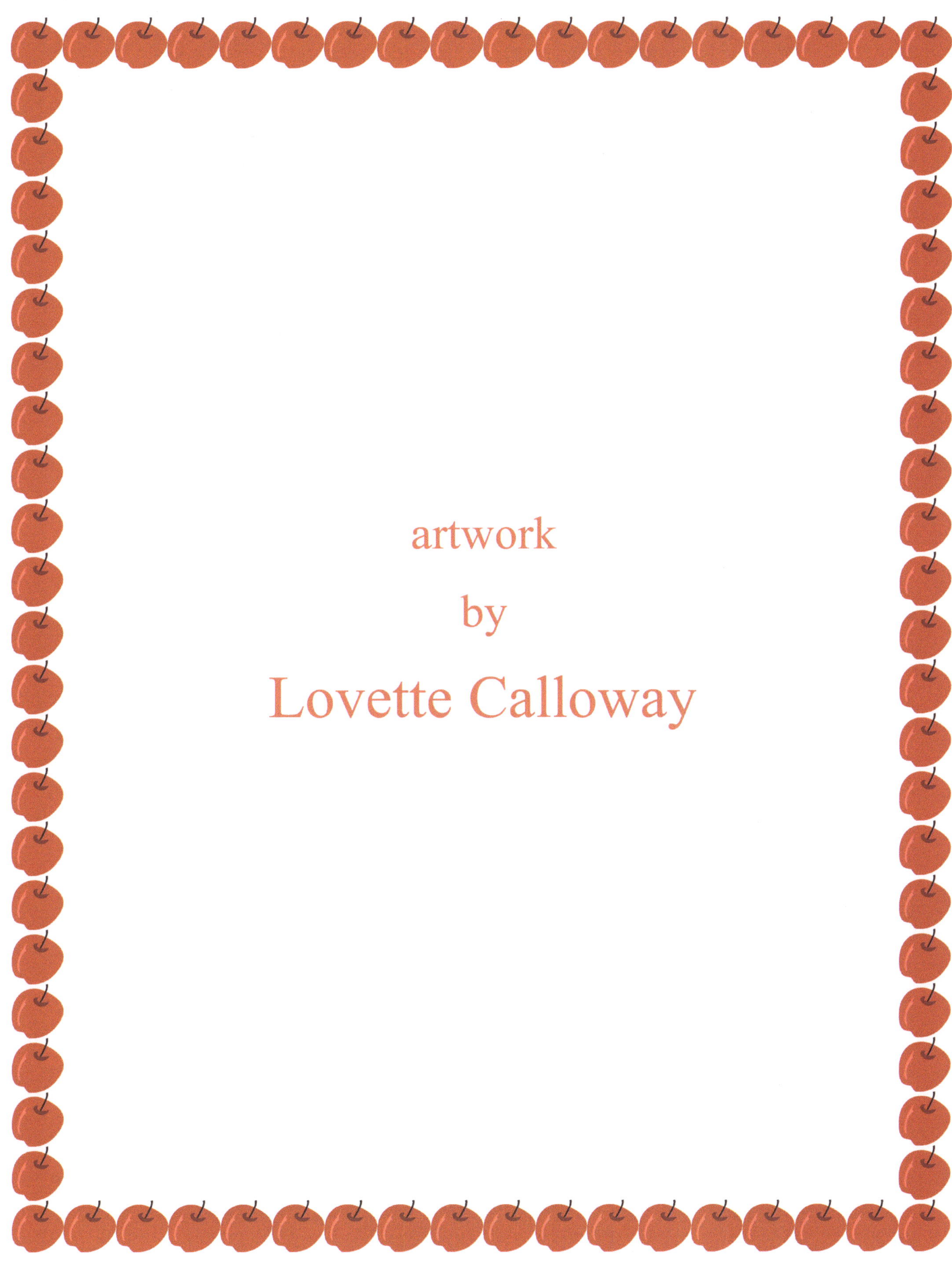

artwork

by

Lovette Calloway

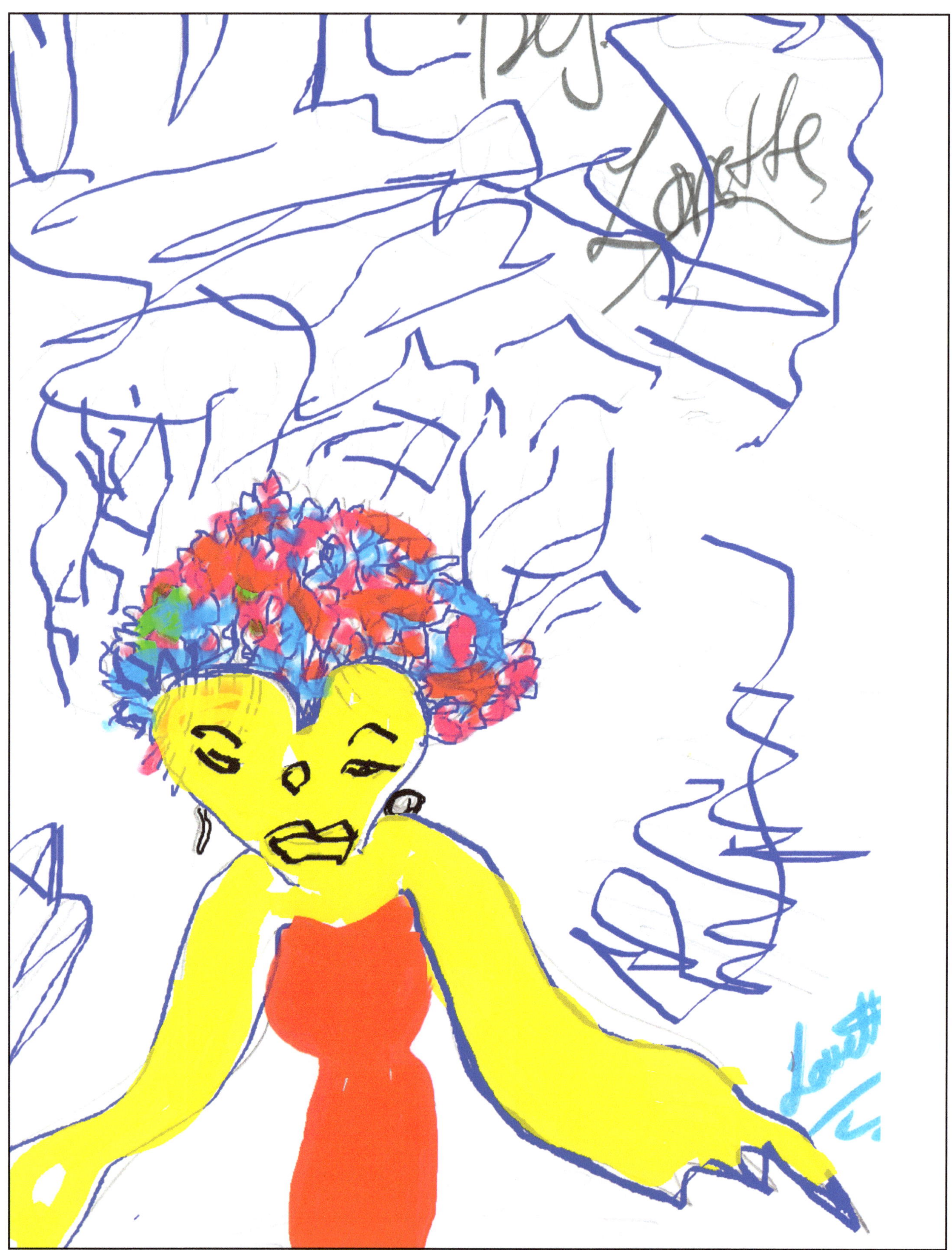

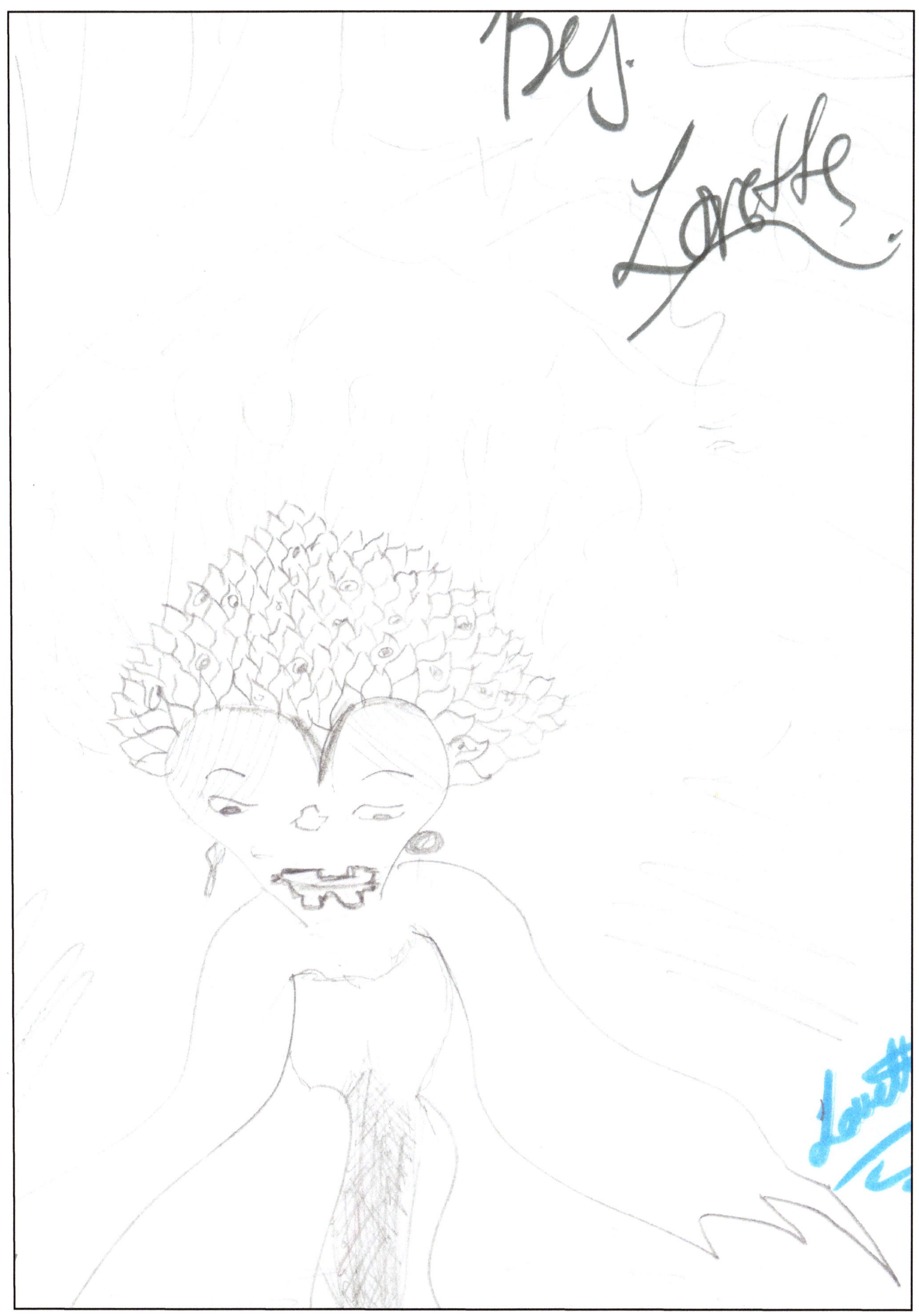
By.

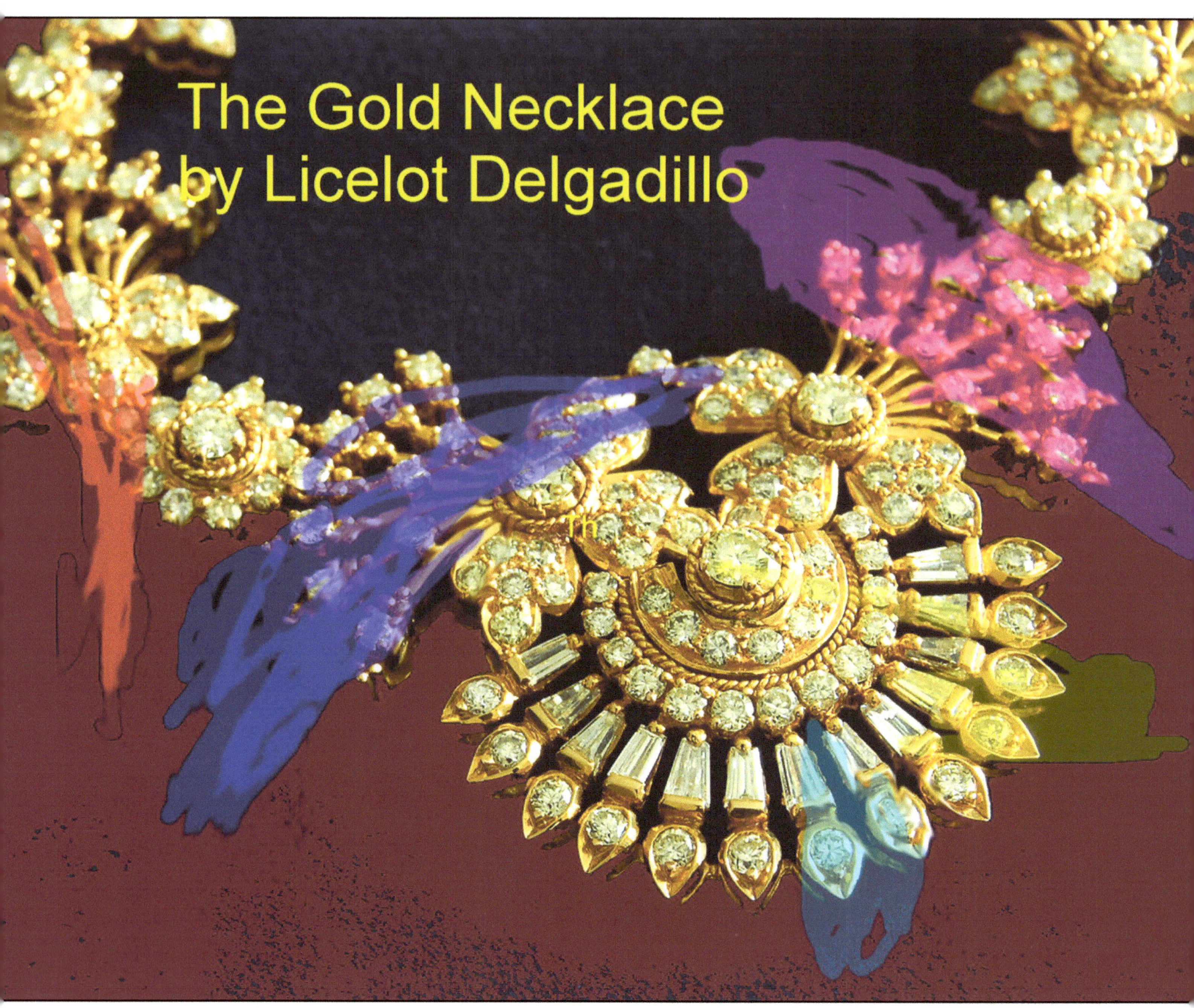
The Gold Necklace
by Licelot Delgadillo

Once upon a time, there was a princess named Krayolah. She was very jumpy, but at the same time very distracted. One day she decided to visit her friend, Jamaica, who lived on the other side of the forest. She hadn't seen her in a very long time so she was very excited about it. Krayolah always wore this beautiful gold necklace that her mother gave her when she was very little. People in town say that this necklace has magical powers because people become angry in the presence of the necklace.

As Krayolah prepares for her journey she has a bad feeling, but she ignores it and continues on. Krayolah decides to take a short cut and ends up in the darkest part of the scary forest. Every step fills her whole body with fear as she walks into the unknown. All of a sudden the necklace starts to glow and Krayolah has no idea why. Then an unknown creature that Krayolah hadn't seen before appears with big eyes, big mouth, big teeth, and enormous arms. The gold necklace makes him even more angry. He stands before Krayolah. She is so scared that she starts melting. At the end, all that is left is a gold necklace in it pool of crayons. The monster goes on to seek more princesses and steal their necklaces...in other words, their youth!

Watch out, he's looking for you!

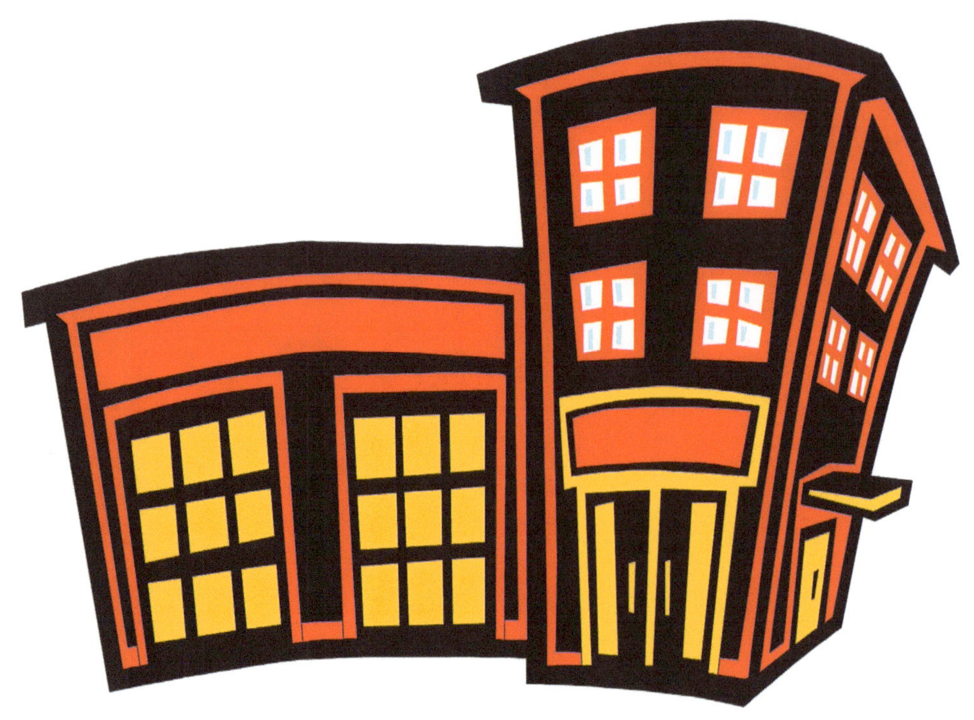

A little bit about the Academy Street Firehouse…

The ARFC is a non-profit organization founded in 1986 by Terry & Faye Zealand with the mission of providing comprehensive services to vulnerable children and families living in New Jersey. Today, the wide array of services include housing, substance abuse prevention, mental and medical health services, and childcare. ARFC's Academy Street Firehouse is an afterschool program uniquely designed to meet the needs of vulnerable at-risk children and adolescents. The Firehouse combines best practices of the youth development and out-of-school-time fields to provide Newark-area students with academic assistance, cultural and artistic enrichment, health and wellness programs, and self-esteem/ team building opportunities. The goal of the Firehouse is to combine holistic services and experiential activities to help at-risk youth build resilient and healthy lives.

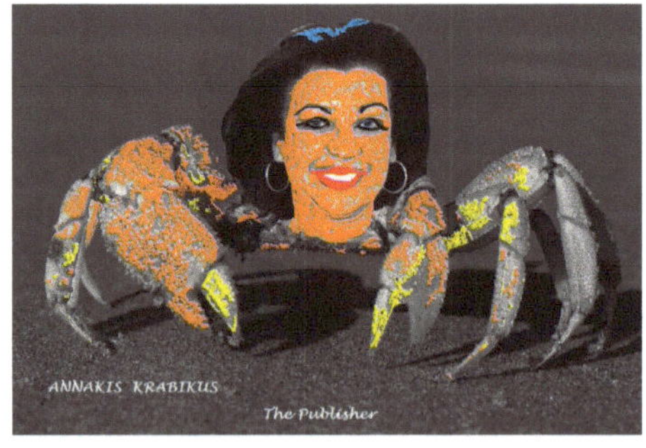

For Inquiries about this book please contact:
Darker Intentions Press
POB 569
Freehold Township, NJ 07728

Book layout provided by Sobee Studio

www.ingramcontent.com/pod-product-compliance
Lightning Source LLC
LaVergne TN
LVHW070147110826
845147LV00002B/338

* 9 7 8 0 9 8 2 7 5 9 7 3 8 *